LOOK WITH THE HEART

Barbara Cartland

Barbara Cartland Ebooks Ltd

This edition © 2021

ISBNs

9781788674348 EPUB

9781788674355 PAPERBACK

Book design by M-Y Books

m-ybooks.co.uk

THE BARBARA CARTLAND ETERNAL COLLECTION

The Barbara Cartland Eternal Collection is the unique opportunity to collect all five hundred of the timeless beautiful romantic novels written by the world's most celebrated and enduring romantic author.

Named the Eternal Collection because Barbara's inspiring stories of pure love, just the same as love itself, the books will be published on the internet at the rate of four titles per month until all five hundred are available.

The Eternal Collection, classic pure romance available worldwide for all time .

THE LATE DAME BARBARA CARTLAND

Barbara Cartland, who sadly died in May 2000 at the grand age of ninety eight, remains one of the world's most famous romantic novelists. With worldwide sales of over one billion, her outstanding 723 books have been translated into thirty six different languages, to be enjoyed by readers of romance globally.

Writing her first book 'Jigsaw' at the age of 21, Barbara became an immediate bestseller. Building upon this initial success, she wrote continuously throughout her life, producing bestsellers for an astonishing 76 years. In addition to Barbara Cartland's legion of fans in the UK and across Europe, her books have always been immensely popular in the USA. In 1976 she achieved the unprecedented feat of having books at numbers 1 & 2 in the prestigious B. Dalton Bookseller bestsellers list.

Although she is often referred to as the 'Queen of Romance', Barbara Cartland also wrote several historical biographies, six autobiographies and numerous theatrical plays as well as books on life, love, health and cookery. Becoming one of Britain's most popular media personalities and dressed in her trademark pink, Barbara spoke on radio and television about social and political issues, as well as making many public appearances.

In 1991 she became a Dame of the Order of the British Empire for her contribution to literature and her work for humanitarian and charitable causes.

Known for her glamour, style, and vitality Barbara Cartland became a legend in her own lifetime. Best remembered for her wonderful romantic novels and loved by millions of readers worldwide, her books remain treasured for their heroic heroes, plucky heroines and traditional values. But above all, it was Barbara Cartland's overriding belief in the positive power of love to help, heal and improve the quality of life for everyone that made her truly unique.

AUTHOR'S NOTE

In my travels all over the world I have met a great many Healers. I talked to one who was 160 years old in the woods in Nepal when I was at the foot of the Himalayas.

There were others beside the Ganges, one near the Diamond Mines in Hyderabad and another in the exquisitely beautiful Lake Palace at Udaipur.

They, all of them, tried to give the Light Force through their hands or their concentration to the person who needs their help.

In this country, the two Healers I found who work in the same way believing in the light that comes from God are Graham Wyley and Joseph Corvo, who is a genius and works on his patients with Zone Therapy.

Fennel was believed to have a great effect on the eyes from the time of the Greeks who not only believed in its effectiveness in healing eyes, but also used it during their Olympic Games as a wreath to put round the head of the Victor.

CHAPTER ONE
1819

Erlina Sherwood stood looking helplessly at the flames soaring higher and higher into the sky.

She could hardly believe that her home was being irretrievably destroyed.

There was a resounding crash as part of the roof fell in and she felt her brother's hand slip into hers.

"I don't think we can save anything more," he sighed.

"No, we must – not go near – it again," Erlina managed to say.

There was just a small number of chairs and pictures, which she and Gerry, who was eleven, had managed to pull into the garden.

As it was in the middle of the night and they were some distance from the village, no one had come to help them.

The old servants, Dawes and his wife, could only stand motionless staring at the flames and weeping.

It was in fact Dawes who had caused the fire.

He had got out of bed in the night and the candle he had left burning by his bedside had toppled over onto the bed.

He did not realise at first that the bedclothes were burning and, when he did, he tried to put out the fire himself.

When the blaze became too strong for him to cope with, his wife ran screaming out of the back door.

It was only then that he hurried as fast as she could through the house to wake Erlina.

He told her what had happened and admitted that it was all his fault.

Erlina quickly woke her brother, who was sleeping in the next room.

They pulled on some clothes and ran rapidly downstairs.

By this time the flames were completely out of control.

Sherwood House was very old, in fact it had been built in Tudor times and the wooden beams and floors were dry and quickly caught fire.

Erlina and Gerry had only managed to bring half a dozen pieces out through the front door and into the garden.

The flames were speedily destroying everything she knew and loved.

Another part of the roof then fell in with a deafening crash.

Then there was just the crackle of the flames with the skeleton of the walls silhouetted against night sky.

"What are we going to do?" Gerry asked.

It was a question that Erlina was already asking herself.

She knew that she had to think of the two old servants as well.

"We will have to drive into the village," she said. "Thank goodness the horses are safe and untouched."

The stables were fortunately built at some distance from the house and it was obvious that the flames would not reach them.

"What shall we do about the Dawes's?" Gerry asked.

"We will take them with us," Erlina replied. "Go and put Nobby between the shafts of the pony cart."

Gerry ran off.

He was only young, but he was a sensible and helpful little boy.

Erlina walked towards the old couple.

"'Tis really terrible – terrible!" the old woman was sobbing. "Everything's been burnt, *everything!*"

Her voice was almost incoherent and Erlina could do nothing but pat her shoulder.

"We have to be brave," she murmured.

"'T'were my fault, miss," Dawes said. "There's no one to blame but me."

"It is something that might have happened at any time," Erlina said consolingly. "The house is so old that I think I always knew that if there was a fire nothing could save it."

Mrs. Dawes was still sobbing and the tears were running down the old cook's cheeks.

Erlina felt like crying herself, but she knew that it would do no good.

"I have sent Master Gerry to fetch the pony cart," she said. "We will then drive into the village and ask the Vicar if we can stay with him for the rest of the night."

She did not wait to hear what the Dawes's had to say, but walked off towards the stables knowing that she must help Gerry.

He had already brought Nobby, who was a most reliable old pony, out of his stall and she helped Gerry fit him between the shafts.

The pony cart was old like everything else they possessed.

She thought despairingly that, unless they were to lay down on the straw with the horses, they would not have a roof over their heads.

"Have you fastened the shaft on your side?" she now asked Gerry.

"I think it is all right," he answered. "It is difficult to see in the dark."

There were stars overhead, but no moon.

Erlina knew, however, that Nobby would find his way over to the Vicarage without any trouble.

She climbed into the pony cart and picked up the reins.

Then, as Gerry would have joined her, she told him,

"Lock the door of the stables. We don't want the horses let out tomorrow if people come up here to look at the fire."

"I don't suppose they will want to walk so far," Gerry commented, "except, of course, for the Vicar and his family."

Erlina did not answer. She only waited while he closed the stable door and had pushed the bolt into place.

Gerry then climbed into the pony cart and Erlina drove carefully out from the stables and down the cobbled way to the front of the house.

The Dawes's were waiting where she had left them, but there was now even less of the house standing than there had been before.

She could not bear to look at it.

She did not want to know that everything she possessed, including all her clothes, would soon be nothing but ashes.

There was just the small number of things that she and Gerry had rescued lying on the grass some way from the fire.

She wished that they had had time to bring the pictures of their ancestors from the dining room and drawing room.

She had always loved the one of her father, who had been the fifth Baronet. Gerry was now the sixth.

Erlina pulled the pony cart to a standstill.

She then told Mr. and Mrs. Dawes to climb in and Gerry jumped out so that Mrs. Dawes could get in first.

She was still crying and Erlina tried to think of something comforting to say.

But the words would not come to her lips.

Gerry told Dawes to sit beside his wife and he sat next to Erlina.

They then drove off down the drive.

Erlina did not want to look back at the blazing building against the dark foliage of the trees behind it.

She could, however, still hear the crackle of the flames and a faint breeze was blowing burning cinders over the lawn.

Then there was only the clip-clop of Nobby's hoofs on the gravelled drive.

When they reached the gates, the fire was out of sight.

Then there were only the stars overhead and, when they turned into it, the darkness of the village with its empty and ruined cottages.

Erlina drove the pony trap on until they came to the grey Norman Church where she had been christened and later confirmed.

Her mother and father were buried in the churchyard in the family vault and it contained all the previous members of the family who had lived in Sherwood House since it was first built.

The Vicarage, which was beside the Church, was only about a hundred years old.

The window frames and doors were badly in need of paint and, as Erlina knew, there was a hole in the roof that had not been repaired.

Gerry rushed out and raised the knocker on the front door.

He knocked twice before a window opened and the Vicar put out his head.

"Who is it?" he asked. "What do you want?"

"It is me, Erlina Sherwood. Our house is on fire and, as we have nowhere to go, we have come to you, Vicar."

"Goodness gracious!" the Reverend Piran Garnet exclaimed. "I will come downstairs at once."

It took some minutes for him to dress before he opened the front door.

The Vicar, a middle-aged man, had always been respected and loved by his parishioners and now there were very few remaining.

As he saw that Gerry was waiting for him on the doorstep, he put his arm round the boy and pulled him close.

"What has happened, Gerry?" he asked.

"The house caught fire, Vicar," Gerry answered, "and already there is almost nothing left – nothing at all."

Erlina thought afterwards that it was characteristic of the Vicar to have taken everything in his stride.

He sent the Dawes's to the kitchen and asked them to make some coffee for Erlina and themselves.

And he found a glass of cider for Gerry to drink.

After Nobby had been put in the stable, they went into the sitting room.

"It was Dawes who accidentally started the fire," Erlina explained to the Vicar, "and he is terribly upset about it. But once the flames had taken a hold in the strong wind, there was nothing that anybody could have done to stop it."

"I can understand that," the Vicar nodded. "I will go up to the house first thing in the morning to see if any of the furniture can be saved."

Erlina shook her head.

"There is no chance of that. Gerry and I managed to carry a few things out of the hall, but it was too dangerous to attempt to rescue anything from any of the rooms."

The Vicar wisely did not let them talk for long.

He took them upstairs and told Gerry to get into bed with one of his two sons.

By taking his daughter into his bed with him and his wife, he provided Erlina with a bed too.

She knew only too well that there were no habitable rooms on the top floor as the roof leaked and there was no one left in the village to do the repairs even if the Vicar had been able to pay for them.

Before Erlina fell asleep from sheer exhaustion, she was wondering despairingly where she and Gerry could go.

How and where would they be able to live in the future?

'Please God – help us," she prayed, "please – *please.*'

*

When Erlina, with dark lines under her eyes, came down for breakfast the next morning she found Gerry already seated at the table.

The Vicar's two children were also there and Mrs. Garnet was bringing in their breakfast from the kitchen.

She put the plates down in front of the children before kissing Erlina.

"I am so sorry," she said, "sorrier than I can possibly say. How can such a dreadful thing have happened to you and Gerry?"

"I have already spoken to old Henry," the Vicar said. "He saw the fire through the trees last night and walked up at dawn to see what had happened."

"That was kind of him," Erlina remarked.

She knew that Henry was an old man from the village who found it difficult to walk far.

"I am afraid he came back with bad news," the Vicar continued. "The fire is subsiding simply because there is now nothing more left to burn."

It was only what Erlina had expected.

At the same time she felt that it was a dagger-thrust in her breast.

"Henry gave the horses water and some food," the Vicar went on, "and told me that the chickens were all right."

Erlina could not even smile her thanks.

"Now don't start worrying until you have had some breakfast," Mrs. Garnet said. "Thank Heaven, we have hens, otherwise we would be starving to death like everyone else who is left in this benighted place!"

As she finished speaking, she walked back into the kitchen.

Erlina looked at the Vicar.

"Have you heard anything from the Marquis?" she asked him in a low voice.

The Vicar shook his head.

"We are living only on what the Bishop can send me out of charity," he replied. "He has written to his Lordship, but there has been no reply."

"I cannot believe it!" Erlina cried. "How can he behave in this appalling manner to you as well as to everyone else in the Parish?"

"I cannot understand it myself," the Vicar agreed, "and Meldon Hall is becoming almost as dilapidated as we are!"

There was no need for him to say anything further.

Erlina had talked and talked about the dreadful conditions in which they were all living and there were no words left to describe the behaviour of the Marquis of Meldon with.

When the old Marquis had died five years ago, his son had come into the title and the large estate. And everyone had expected things to go on as they always had in the past.

It had only been a question of when the new Marquis would come back to his home.

He would, they thought, reorganise the lives of the villagers as his father and grandfather had done before him.

Practically every man and woman worked in some capacity on the estate or in the 'Big House' as had always happened in so many villages throughout the country.

After six months had passed everybody began to be even more apprehensive.

And they asked nervously what was going on at Meldon Hall.

First of all, there was no sign of the Marquis.

Then Mr. Cranley, who had been the Manager in charge of the house and the estate for years, began to give the workers notice to leave.

"What's 'appening? Why be us sent away?" they asked him indignantly.

Because it was so traditional, their fathers, their grandfathers and their great-grandfathers had all worked at Meldon over many years.

It was extremely difficult for Mr. Cranley, who was a kindly and warm-hearted man.

He had to explain that the new Marquis had no intention of spending any money on his estate.

He also would not keep any servants in the house, which he did not intend to visit at any time.

"But why? Why?" everybody asked forlornly over and over again.

Mr. Cranley could give them no explanation whatsoever.

Then, as a year passed by and then another, all the able men had left the village in search of jobs.

They had to find work elsewhere to keep themselves and their wives and children.

What was more, the cottages, which desperately needed repair, began to fall down from endless neglect.

Finally, after five years, there was hardly anyone left in the village except for four men who worked for Sir Richard Sherwood.

Then they too began to leave after he become so desperately ill.

"'Tis just like this, miss," they explained to Erlina, 'Our friends 'ave gone and there be nowhere in the village now the inn's closed where us can even stop and 'ave a drink."

"I know that," Erlina replied, "but we need you. How can we work our land if you are not here?"

"I understands your feelings, miss," one man said, "but the Missus says 'er's not walkin' two miles for a shop and you knows as Mister Geary's gone broke."

There was nothing that Erlina could say to comfort any of them.

She had wished despairingly that her father was well enough to even talk with the men.

But Sir Richard was a dying man because he had suffered a severe stroke for no apparent reason when he had seemed so fit and vigorous.

When he did die, she was left with Gerry to look after and the Dawes's who had nowhere else to go even if they wanted to.

They stayed on in the house that Erlina loved and which had always been her home.

It was so heart-breaking to see the garden going to rack and ruin and to realise that their four hundred acres of land was now growing nothing but weeds.

It meant too that she and Gerry had very little income to live on.

Now that he was eleven, she knew that in a year's time he ought to be going to Eton as it was where their father had been educated and most of their relations.

She would lie awake night after night wondering what on earth she could do.

Then in the morning she would struggle to keep the house clean and she had to drive nearly two miles to buy the small amount of food that they could actually afford.

She kept asking herself how they could go on like this, but could not find an answer.

The Garnets at the Vicarage were the only people who she could talk to.

But they could find no solution for their own problems let alone those of anyone else.

Every time Erlina drove through the village and could see the abandoned cottages and their weed-filled gardens, she hated the Marquis more and more.

It was quite impossible to tell him what she felt as he had not deigned even to answer the plaintive letters written to him by the Vicar.

It was Mrs. Garnet who was most voluble about it.

"The man is a murderer, that is what he is!" she said when she and Erlina were alone. "I know that the old people would have lived longer if they had kept their pensions and, if my husband did not receive a pittance from the Bishop, we too would starve to death!"

"Surely something can be done?" Erlina asked her.

"My husband thought of going up to London and speaking to the Marquis himself," Mrs. Garnet said. "But it would be very expensive and I doubt if his Lordship would even trouble himself to see him!"

"Why is he behaving like this?" Erlina enquired.

"That is what we are all asking," she replied. "There is plenty written in the newspapers about him enjoying himself, racing his horses at Newmarket, hunting in Leicestershire and attending parties given by the Prince Regent, all of which cost thousands and thousands of pounds."

Erlina knew that Mrs. Garnet had a sister who lived in London and she would send her the newspapers from time to time and this was why she knew so much about the Marquis's movements.

The more Erlina heard about him, the more she felt that he must be growing horns like the Devil himself.

He so obviously never gave a thought to the people who had always depended upon his family for employment and their pensions when they grew older.

"I hate him! *I hate him*!" she would say night after night.

But she was quite certain that, however violent her feelings were, they would not disturb the 'Wicked Marquis'.

Now as Mrs. Garnet came back to the breakfast table to put a poached egg in front of Erlina, she said to her husband,

"Have you thought of where Erlina and Gerry can go? Much as we love them, you know, Piran, there is no room fit for them to stay here in the Vicarage."

"I am aware of that," the Vicar said quietly, "and there is only one place that they can go."

"Where can that be?" Erlina asked him with some surprise in her voice.

She did not believe that he could be clever enough to find somewhere suitable for her and Gerry.

"Mr. Cranley must accommodate them at The Hall," the Vicar responded.

If he had dropped a bomb on the table, Erlina could not have been more surprised.

"Do you mean – Meldon Hall?" she gasped.

"Why not? As you are well aware, there is really nowhere else," the Vicar said. "There is not a cottage in the village that does not have leaks and, while we would love to have you, you know yourself that there is no room here unless you sleep on the floor."

"I think that is a very sensible suggestion," Mrs. Garnet said. "After all, Mr. Cranley is alone in that big house as he has been for the last five years and so he has had to look after himself since Lucy died."

Lucy had been the last remaining servant, Erlina knew, who had stayed on at The Hall after all the other servants had been given notice to leave.

She was crippled with arthritis, had no relatives who anyone knew about and nowhere else to go.

She had been the Marquis's nursery maid when he was a small boy and then, when Mr. Cranley had told her that she had to leave, she had answered him firmly,

"This be my home and the only way I'll be leavin' here be in a coffin!"

Mr. Cranley had not been able to pay her anything and he himself received only a very small wage from the Marquis's Solicitors. And this was for acting as caretaker at Meldon Hall and managing the estate what was left of it.

It was the same money that he had received twenty years earlier when he had first gone there and he had hoped when the new Marquis took over that it would be increased.

What had happened was that his wages did arrive, but now he had to pay for his food and anything else that he required, which he had not had to do in the past.

He had stayed on because, as for Lucy, it had become his home and he had nowhere else to go as well.

Erlina had often thought that it was a miserable and lonely existence for him.

Mr. Cranley was an educated man who had served the family to the best of his ability for more than twenty years.

He had then been left to a life of loneliness on what was almost a starvation diet.

Still the house was there and, as she thought about it, Erlina just knew that the Vicar was right.

"It will give you a respite, Erlina," he said now, "to write to your relatives and tell them what has happened. I feel sure that one of them will be able to take you in."

"I very much doubt it," Erlina answered. "As you know, Papa's brothers and sisters are all dead.

The few cousins that are left live in Yorkshire and I think there are two still alive in Cornwall."

The Vicar knew without her saying anything more that she and Gerry certainly could not afford to travel such long distances.

"The first thing that you have to do is to have somewhere to sleep," he said in a practical voice, "and after that we must think about your future."

"You are so kind to me," Erlina smiled.

She had noticed while they had been talking that Mrs. Garnet had no egg for breakfast and she was eating only toast with a thin scraping of butter.

She knew only too well that she and Gerry must not impose on their hospitality.

Yet she had never imagined for one moment that she might live at Meldon Hall, which was an enormous house.

It had been largely re-built in the last century and it was most impressive to look at from all directions.

Yet Erlina had heard that the whole top floor of the house was now uninhabitable.

In several of the State bedrooms, the ceilings had fallen in through years of untreated damp.

At the same time the structure of the building was strong and resilient.

It would take very much longer to destroy it than the cottages, which had all collapsed within five years or less without any attention or repairs.

The village inn, once it was closed, had quickly begun to fall into decay.

Aloud she now said,

"You are quite right, Vicar. Gerry and I will go up to The Hall and ask Mr. Cranley to take us in. At least we will have plenty of room there to move about in."

She tried to speak bravely and with a smile.

But the tears were very near to the surface as she thought that she would never again be able to go home.

She drank a little coffee.

Then she said,

"I suppose I had better take the Dawes's with me as well."

"There is nowhere for them to stay in the village," the Vicar said, "and they might be useful in cleaning up The Hall."

"Mrs. Dawes is a good cook when she has any of the ingredients," Erlina answered, "so perhaps Mr. Cranley would be pleased to have her there."

She was hoping that this would be the case as there was nowhere else suitable in the vicinity.

So if Mr. Cranley refused to let them stay in the house where he was still in charge, they would have to sleep on hay bales in the stables with the horses and there was, she told herself, literally no other place for them.

Mrs. Garnet began to clear away the plates and the Vicar's children had not left a crumb.

When Erlina looked at them, she felt that, attractive though they were, they were all three of them far too thin.

The Vicar too looked older than his age.

She felt her hatred for the Marquis well up inside her again and she wanted to denounce him as she had often done before.

Then she asked herself what was the point? He was impervious to anything that might be said of him.

It was therefore only poetic justice that she and Gerry should take shelter under his roof when they had nowhere else to go.

As the Vicar rose from his chair, she said,

"We will go up to The Hall now – and thank you a million times for being so kind to us."

The Vicar put his hand on her shoulder.

"I wish I could do more," he said, "but you know how difficult things are at present."

"Of course I know," Erlina answered, "and I only hope that the wicked, wicked Marquis burns in a special Hell that is kept for people as bad as he is!"

The Vicar's eyes twinkled.

Then, as he kissed Erlina's cheek, he said,

"You know quite well that I cannot say 'Amen' to that."

They both laughed and somehow it broke the tension.

"I think it's just spiffing that we are going to The Hall," Gerry piped up. "I have always wanted to explore those big big rooms, but you would not let me."

"You will have your chance now," Erlina said, "and Goodness knows what we may find."

"I expect it is full of ghosts!" Gerry said. "If Tom comes to see me tomorrow, we will play Hide and Seek."

Tom Garnet was about the same age as Gerry and looked pleased at the idea.

"I would like that," he said. "May I go, Papa?"

"I can see no reason why not," the Vicar replied.

Then he turned to Erlina.

"You had better not give Mr. Cranley too much of a shock," he said, "so I will send Tom up to play with Gerry as soon as you are settled in."

"I want to go too," Tom said, who was little more than one year younger than Gerry.

"And me! And me!" Helen cried, who was only five.

"We shall all go later," the Vicar promised, "but you must understand that we cannot go today."

The children looked disappointed, but they were very obedient and respectful.

"I cannot come to see you this afternoon," the Vicar said to Erlina, "as I have promised my wife that I will take her to the shop in the next village."

He paused for a moment to clear his throat and then continued,

"But I will come tomorrow and then perhaps we can make arrangements as to how Gerry is to continue with his lessons."

Erlina had been teaching her brother in the best way that she could. It was the Vicar, however, who had taught him Latin and arithmetic besides giving him an interest in literature.

It had been an excellent arrangement.

Erlina, however, was always uncomfortably conscious that they should be paying for his tuition.

As that was impossible, she could only express how grateful she was to the Vicar over and over again.

"I know that Gerry will have no difficulties in getting into Eton," she had said only last week.

She had been wondering constantly how she would ever be able to find enough money to pay for the school fees.

She just hoped that by some miracle something would happen before next September and that was when he was due to take his entrance tests.

She had thought that the only possibility was to ignore the fact that the best pictures in the house were entailed onto Gerry's son when he had one.

The Trustees, who were supposed to see that the pictures were not sold, had not called at Sherwood House to inspect them for over three years now.

They were getting old and it was a long journey for each of them to undertake.

'It may be cheating,' Erlina had said to herself, 'but what is the point of a picture on the wall if Gerry is unable to go to Eton?'

She therefore renewed her efforts to teach him herself and she had been more grateful than ever to the Vicar for doing the same.

She could not help feeling that the large library that she knew Meldon Hall contained would be of tremendous help to Gerry with his studies if to nobody else.

She had never been in The Hall and her father had not been particularly friendly with the last Marquis.

He naturally met him occasionally on committees in the County and at social gatherings such as local Race Meetings.

But the Marchioness had considered that she was too grand to bother with people in the County. With, of course, the exception of the Lord Lieutenant.

She had therefore not included Sir Richard and Lady Sherwood in any of her parties or special occasions.

She had in fact spent more time in Meldon House in London than she did at Meldon Hall.

It was only the old Marquis who, during the last few years of his life, had stayed put in the country and refused to leave it.

Erlina could remember seeing the present Marquis, when he was a youth, riding through the village.

She had never met him and he was eight years older than she was.

This meant that, as she was now nineteen, he would be twenty-seven.

He was, she thought bitterly, old enough to know how to behave.

*

Climbing into the pony cart, Erlina and Gerry waved goodbye to the Garnets.

As Erlina drove up the mile long drive that led to Meldon Hall, she could not suppress a little thrill of excitement.

She had seen the building from a distance, but only because she had taken the liberty of riding a little way up the drive. As she peeped at the magnificent house it had seemed to her a mystery house simply because she had never been inside it to see for herself.

Her father and mother had not been in the least perturbed at not being accepted by the Meldons.

Lady Sherwood had had a very sweet and gentle disposition.

She had never said an unkind word about anybody and she was also somewhat shy and reserved. She had no desire to push herself onto people who she thought were more at home in London Society than in the country.

She was, however, an excellent rider, just as she had taught her children to be and she was happiest when she was riding with her husband over their own land.

In the winter they hunted with a small pack nearby that was certainly not smart enough for the Meldons.

When her mother was alive, Erlina had felt that the house was always filled with laughter and love.

Sometimes they had friends to stay, but most of the time they were alone and enjoying their own company

But there had always seemed to be more than enough to do and life was very amenable.

She had been only sixteen when her mother had died and then her father fell ill shortly afterwards.

It was then that the days had seemed long and the evenings more and more lonely.

When she and Gerry were finally alone, it was very frightening. By this time the village was dying too and she felt sometimes as if a great black cloud had descended over them.

It seemed to be coming closer and closer until she had the feeling that she herself would be swallowed up.

The cause of it, of course, was the appalling behaviour of the 'Wicked Marquis'.

It was he who had put an evil spell on everyone from which they could not escape.

CHAPTER TWO

Erlina pulled Nobby up at the bottom of the long flight of steps that led to the front door of Meldon Hall.

To her surprise she saw that the door was open.

"I tell you what we will do," she said to Gerry. "You drive Nobby into the stable yard and Dawes and Mrs. Dawes can go into the house through the kitchen entrance. I expect the door will be open."

Gerry nodded as she went on,

"I will go in and find Mr. Cranley. Then I will come and help you unharness Nobby."

"All right," Gerry agreed readily.

He always enjoyed driving the old pony.

As soon as Erlina climbed out of the pony cart he drove off slowly towards the stables.

Erlina ran up the steps thinking that this was the crucial moment.

If she could not persuade Mr. Cranley to let them all stay in the house, where could they possibly go?

She walked into the hall and was aware that the stairs and furniture were thick with dust.

So was the mantelpiece where stood a number of very fine china ornaments.

She stopped gazing around her and started to wonder where Mr. Cranley would be at this time of the day.

In the old days she suspected that he would have had an office where he would pay the wages and the bills and have the walls covered with maps of the estate.

There would certainly be no point in his sitting in this room now.

She walked into the hall and looked into the room on the right. The shutters were closed and it was in darkness.

She next went across the hall to the other side.

She saw as she walked through the door that on one of the windows the shutter had been opened. And the deep Georgian glass window had been opened as well. The rest of the room was in darkness and then she called out,

"Are you there, Mr. Cranley?"

There was no answer and she was about to turn away and look elsewhere when a man's voice called out to her unexpectedly,

"He has gone to the village."

Erlina started, wondering who it could be.

"How annoying," she said, "I must have only just missed him. I expect he went over the Park and I came up the drive."

There was no reply.

She thought that the man must be at the other end of the room and she went on as if she was speaking to herself,

"Anyway if he does go to the Vicarage, the Vicar will tell him where I am and about the ghastly – terrible thing that has – happened to me and Gerry."

Even as she spoke the horror of the fire seemed to sweep over her yet again.

Then the man who had spoken before asked,

"What has happened to have upset you so much?"

"Anyone would – be upset," Erlina replied, "if the house in which they – lived had been – burnt to the – ground!"

"That must indeed have been a dreadful shock to you," the voice agreed.

"It was ghastly, frightening and – now I must – speak to Mr. Cranley."

"Why?"

Because she could not see the man, she did not feel that he was being inquisitive.

She answered him as if it was somebody she knew and who would understand her plight.

"My brother and I, and the old servants who – live with us, have simply nowhere else to – go."

"Surely there must be a cottage in the village where you could stay?" the man suggested.

"In the village?" she echoed. "You must be a – stranger in – these parts and Mr. Cranley cannot have – told you that the – village is dead."

She paused for a moment and then continued,

"It has died because the – wicked – cruel – evil Marquis has murdered it and – all the – people who – lived there,"

She spoke violently.

Her feelings on what had happened seemed even more intense than they had been when she had woken up that morning.

It was as if the numbness that had swept over her as she watched the deadly fire burning everything she possessed had now evaporated.

Instead she was feeling the sheer horror of it all much more intensely than before.

"I cannot quite understand what you are saying," the stranger remarked.

"It is – quite simple," Erlina replied. "The Marquis, who, as I expect you know, owns this house, sacked all the – people who worked on Meldon Estate."

She then continued more slowly.

"They had to go away to seek work – elsewhere. The old people received no – pensions and – died from – lack of food and the – cold and rain – which sank into their – cottages as they were – never repaired."

"I don't believe that what I am hearing is true," the stranger expostulated.

"Unfortunately it is the truth," Erlina insisted. "My father did what he could, but then – the men who – worked for us – left too."

"Why did they do that?"

"Because there were no longer any shops in the village where they could buy food – and even – the inn closed so that there was – nowhere for them to go for their – ale and cider. So when there was – no one left to – work on our land, we also found it – hard to stay alive."

She gave a deep sigh.

"Your father, if he owned an estate, must have had money," the stranger argued.

Again Erlina, deep in her thoughts, did not really feel that she was now talking to a living person.

He was anonymous and she could not even see him. It was therefore almost as if she was answering the questions herself that came into her own mind.

"We had money during the War," she said, "when, of course – our crops fetched – good prices in the market."

She hesitated for a moment to catch her breath and then continued,

"But I expect you know that, when peace was restored, the farmers had to compete with cheap food coming into England from the Continent. Many of the country Banks closed their doors. Ours was – one of – them."

She gave a little sob before she went on,

"Then my father – died. He had been very – generous with what he could afford – but there was hardly enough – left to keep Gerry and me from – s-starving."

She tripped on the last word and then went on,

"That is what is – happening now to – the Vicar. That wicked 'Wicked Marquis' has not paid his – stipend and his children are – thin and hungry. All he has to – rely on is what the Bishop gives – him out of charity."

As she spoke the last words, she found that tears were running down her cheeks.

She walked to the window so as to hide them from the man, whoever he might be, who was talking to her.

She had not cried last night when Dawes had burnt down their house and now the tears could not be controlled although she did her best to wipe them away.

There was a long silence while the man in the shadows did not speak.

Then at last he said,

"Can you really be attributing all this misery to one man?"

Erlina wiped her eyes again with her handkerchief and the knuckles of her left hand.

"He is – responsible for – everything," she declared. "I was – saying this morning that I hope he suffers in a special – Hell as – we have all suffered and I was – thinking how – stupid it was of my father to have – saved his life when – he was a boy."

There was no reply again from the stranger.

As if she felt that she should justify the accusation, she carried on,

"He was riding over a stream that had swollen in the heavy winter rains when his pony stumbled and threw him. He was swept away and would have – drowned if my father had not plunged from his horse into the water and saved him."

"And who was your father?" the stranger then asked.

"His name was Sir Richard Sherwood," Erlina answered, "and if he had let the 'Wicked Marquis' drown a great number of – villagers would still be – alive today."

Again there was silence before the man in the shadows said,

"If I remember rightly the Sherwood Estate marches with this one – and I have often wondered who it was who saved me from the flood in the stream."

For a moment Erlina did not understand what he had said.

Then she stiffened and very slowly turned round.

"Are you – saying," she asked, "that – "

Even as she spoke there was the sound of footsteps outside and Gerry came to the door shouting,

"Erlina! Erlina! Where are you?"

"I-I am – here," Erlina managed to reply.

Gerry came into the room.

"What do you think?" he asked. "There are some spiffing horses in the stables and the grooms told me that they belong to the Marquis. Do you think he is here?"

Erlina looked towards the darker part of the room.

She could vaguely see that there was someone sitting in one of the armchairs in front of the fireplace.

"Wh-who are – you? Is it possible – " she stammered, "can it be – true that you are – ?"

" – the 'Wicked Marquis'!" the stranger finished.

"I-I don't – know what – to say," Erlina murmured. "How could I have – known that you would – return here without anyone – knowing that you were coming?"

"I came because it suited me to do so," the Marquis answered. "But I had no idea that my absence had caused so much chaos if what you have been telling me is the truth."

"Of course it is true," Erlina said, "and I have often thought – how much I would like to – tell you what a – terrible state everything is in – but you never – answered the letters that the Vicar – wrote to you – nor I would imagine – those from Mr. Cranley."

"I realise now that it was a mistake," the Marquis remarked slowly, "but I so wished to forget this house and everything that went with it."

"But – how could you have been – so cruel? How could – you have – let all those – old people die?"

"That is something I did not intend," the Marquis answered. "In fact I was not thinking of the village or of the people who lived there but just of The Hall itself."

"How could you not – understand that the – people were brought up to – believe that – Meldon Hall was everything that mattered in – their lives? In fact they had – no life apart from it."

There was silence.

Then Gerry asked in a loud whisper,

"Is that really the Marquis sitting over there?"

"Yes, it is," the Marquis answered.

"You have some ripping horses," Gerry enthused admiringly. "If I could ride horses like those, I would never want to do anything else."

Erlina was trying to pierce the darkness to see what the Marquis looked like.

Then in a very small voice she stammered,

"I-I suppose – you want us to – go away – but we have nowhere else to – go."

"You said we were going to stay here," Gerry protested. "But if not, where can we go unless we sleep in the stables at home."

"That – is the – truth," Erlina whispered.

She walked across the room.

"Please, your Lordship, please let us stay here for just a – few days until we can think of – somewhere else where – we can go."

"I cannot imagine why anyone should want to stay here as it is," he replied. "However I hope to have some servants soon."

"Servants?" Erlina repeated. "But there are none available – in the village."

Then she gave a little cry.

"Oh, but perhaps you will let the Dawes help you. We have brought them with us. Mrs. Dawes is an excellent cook and Dawes knows his duties as a butler and will, I am sure, look – better when he is – having more to eat."

"I suppose I am responsible for that too," the Marquis commented.

"You will not – like my saying so – but it is the – truth," Erlina answered.

To her surprise there came a laugh from the other side of the room.

"I may as well be hanged for a sheep as a lamb!" the Marquis said. "But I will certainly take the Dawes's in and anybody else who can provide for me."

There was a poignant silence.

Then Erlina said hesitatingly,

"As Gerry and – I have nothing left except for the – clothes we stand up in – and there are only a few – pounds left in the Bank – we will work for you – if you will have us."

"And what do you suggest you could do for me?" the Marquis enquired.

Erlina made a little gesture with her hands.

"Anything you – might require, my Lord. I can be your – housekeeper until you can find – someone more experienced, which – might be rather difficult in this – part of the world. Or I could – clean your house as I have been cleaning – our own since – my father died."

"Very well then, Miss Sherwood," the Marquis agreed. "You can run the house for me and help Cranley engage what servants he can find."

"You are not – thinking of bringing – any from London?" Erlina asked him.

"No!"

The monosyllable was sharp and Erlina realised that the suggestion had annoyed him.

Gerry, who had been listening to the conversation, then said,

"I don't know what I can do unless I help look after the horses, my Lord."

"How old are you?" the Marquis asked.

"I am eleven and three months," Gerry replied. "But I am very strong."

"Then I certainly think you should help with the horses and exercise them," the Marquis said.

"Do you mean – ride them?"

"If you are a good rider."

Gerry gave a whoop of joy.

"I am a very very good rider, my Lord. Tell him, Erlina, tell him how good I am."

"I have always considered that you are excellent," Erlina said, "but then we have not had very well-bred horses."

"I will be very careful with your horses," Gerry promised, "and thank you, thank you for saying I can ride them."

He turned towards the door.

"I will just go and have another look at them," he said. "The grooms are grumbling that the stables want cleaning and there are tiles off the roof."

He went from the room and the Marquis said in an amused voice,

"I suppose that is my fault too!"

"There have been no repairs done to the house any more than there have in the village," Erlina replied. "I have heard, although I have not seen it myself, that the roof is in a bad state and the ceilings have fallen in some of the State rooms."

"It will be your job, Miss Sherwood," the Marquis said, "to ensure that they are repaired as quickly as possible."

"Do you – really mean that?" Erlina asked. "Are you seriously going – to let Gerry and me live here, my Lord?"

"Despite the fact that you are frightened and look at me in horror," the Marquis replied, "that is what I intend."

"But why?" Erlina asked. "Why should you suddenly have changed – your mind after all – these years of not even – communicating with – anybody?"

The Marquis did not reply and she went on,

"Mr. Cranley has had – a struggle to keep – alive on the very small wage he is being – paid as – caretaker and after Lucy died – you remember Lucy?"

She paused before she added,

"He has been – alone in this – big house and could not – afford even to have anyone – clean it, even if there had been – anybody left in the – village who would do so."

The Marquis was silent.

And then Erlina thought that she had been rude.

He might change his mind about letting them stay so she added quickly,

"I had better – start by opening – the shutters, my Lord. It is depressing to sit here in the dark."

"You may open the shutters," he replied, "but it will make no difference to me."

Erlina had already gone to one of the other windows and, pulling back the shutters, said over her shoulder,

"Why should it make no difference?"

There was no answer.

She opened the shutters wide and the sunlight came streaming into the room.

There were two more windows to open, but already she could see clearly.

She looked across to where the Marquis was sitting by the fireplace.

As she did so, she gave a little cry.

Covering his eyes was a black bandage.

"Oh!" she exclaimed. "I did not realise – I had no idea – "

"That I am blind?" the Marquis said. "Now you will understand why I have come home."

The way he spoke made her answer perceptively,

"Because you did not wish to be seen."

"Exactly," he agreed, "the oculist told me that I am to keep my eyes bandaged and be completely in the dark if there is to be any chance of my seeing again."

"I am sorry – very sorry, it must be – terrible for you."

"It is the Hell that you have been wishing me to suffer."

Erlina was silent for a moment.

Then she asked him,

"How did it – happen? Did you have an – accident?"

"The bough of a tree hit me across the eyes when I was taking part in a Steeplechase at night."

"Was that not – rather dangerous?"

"It was *very* dangerous," he agreed. "The riders had their left arms bound to their sides, and were all blind drunk!"

"I have heard of these Steeplechases taking place amongst the bucks and beaux," Erlina said, "and I always thought it a – very silly and – life threatening thing to do."

"It was a challenge," the Marquis responded defensively.

"You might have – killed yourself," Erlina murmured.

"One of the competitors in fact was killed and another was severely injured."

"How could you have been so – stupid, my Lord? Just how could you – risk what, after all – is the most – precious possession you have – your life?"

"I did not think of that at the time," the Marquis said, "but, of course, Miss Sherwood, you are quite right."

He spoke in a mocking rather cynical manner.

Because it made Erlina feel somewhat embarrassed, she returned to the next window and started to release the shutters.

"It is unnecessary to go to all that trouble," the Marquis said. "All I can see is darkness, darkness, darkness! You are quite right, Miss Sherwood, it is an unmitigated Hell!"

Erlina sighed.

Now she could see him clearly, she realised that he was an extremely handsome man.

His hair was swept back from a square forehead and, despite the black bandage, she could see that he had fine features and a square rather aggressive chin.

He was dressed in the height of fashion with an intricately tied white cravat.

He wore a whipcord coat over a champagne-coloured waistcoat that matched closely his pantaloons.

His boots shone as if, as Erlina had heard but had not believed, they had been cleaned with champagne.

She stood for a moment looking at him.

Then she said very quietly,

"If you are to get well, which, my Lord, of course you want to do, you have to believe that this is only a – temporary affliction."

"Are you preaching at me?" the Marquis asked.

"I am trying hard to make you understand that good health has not only to do with our physical body, but also our mind and, although you may not like the word – our soul."

"I thought you were very certain that I did not have one," the Marquis instantly argued.

"It should be a – challenge to prove that I am wrong," Erlina said quickly and saw the smile on his lips.

"Can you really be concerned, after all you have said, with my wellbeing?" the Marquis asked.

Again there was that mocking note in his voice that he had used before.

"As your employee, my Lord," Erlina replied, "it is my – duty to be concerned with your food and your wellbeing – and that is what I hope you will be paying me to do."

She thought as she spoke that perhaps she was being somewhat outrageous in what she was saying.

At the same time the words seemed to come to her lips without her thinking out what she should say.

Again the Marquis laughed.

"You are making my homecoming very different from what I had expected a short while ago."

Erlina walked to the last window.

"Without wishing to be in the least impertinent," she asked, "I am very – very – curious as to why you have not come – home before."

"Do you really want to know?" the Marquis enquired.

She opened the fourth window thinking that the sunshine and the fresh air would sweep away the mustiness in the room.

Then she walked back to the fireplace and, as she knew that he could not see her, she sat down in an armchair near to his.

She suddenly felt as if the shock of what had just happened made it difficult for her legs to support her.

And yet he was so different from anything that she might have expected that she wanted to go on talking to the Marquis.

He was not looking quite as frightening as she had expected he would and, when she had thought of him before and had positively hated him, he had seemed to her a personification of the Devil.

Now she could only imagine how frustrating it really must be for a young man who was obviously very athletic to be completely blind.

The black bandage looked as if it had been wound very tightly round his head, but she was sure that the oculist had insisted on it. If it was at all loose, it might let in the light at the sides and this could easily worsen his chances of recovering his sight.

"Do you really want to know why I have done all those things that you have condemned me for?" the Marquis asked. "It was because I was so desperately unhappy here when I was your brother's age."

"Unhappy?" Erlina exclaimed.

It was something that she could never have imagined.

"My mother never seemed to be very fond of me," the Marquis went on, "and my father was a martinet. He believed that children should be treated as if they were raw recruits to be bullied and whipped into unquestioning obedience until they had no will of their own."

"And that – really happened to – you?" Erlina asked.

"I used to cry myself to sleep every night that I was here," the Marquis answered. "The only time

I could escape from what seemed to be persecution by my father was when I was at boarding school."

He paused for a moment to cough before he continued,

"I dreaded the holidays. I used to have a sinking feeling inside me as I came up the drive and the moment I stepped into the hall I felt sick with apprehension about what would happen when my father saw me."

"I was aware that my father never liked yours," Erlina said, "and your mother did not think we were grand enough to know. But, of course, I had no idea that anything like that was happening. We were always so very happy in our house."

"Mine was like a prison, a torture chamber. It burned itself into my mind so that once I was old enough I vowed revenge on what to me had been a place of misery."

Erlina sighed.

"Now I can understand why you acted the way you did. But surely, when you received letters from the Vicar and other people, I suppose they told you what the situation was, you had some idea tghen of what you were allowing to happen on your estate?"

"To be truthful I never read the letters," the Marquis admitted. "They were opened by my secretary and, when he said the words, 'Meldon

Hall', I instructed him to throw them into the wastepaper basket."

"If only we had – understood that was how – you were – feeling," Erlina said in a low voice.

"Would it have made things any better?" the Marquis quizzed her.

"I suppose – not," she confessed, "but everything has been so – ghastly this last year or so with nobody left in the village except for just a few old people who are incapable of going anywhere else."

She was thinking of Henry as she spoke and she knew that there were two other old men and an old woman who was too weak to leave her bed.

The Vicar himself had put tarpaulins over the roofs of their cottages to keep out the rain and they had somehow managed to survive although they were all very feeble.

"What are you going to do now?" she asked him.

As if the Marquis had followed her thoughts, he said,

"You have forced me, Miss Sherwood, into accepting one challenge. I suppose therefore that I shall have to accept another one."

"What do you mean by that?" Erlina asked him feeling perplexed.

"I daresay," he said sarcastically, "you are only too willing and able to tell me what I have to do.

Although I cannot resurrect the dead, I can do something for those who are still living."

Erlina drew in her breath.

"Do you – mean that? Do you – really mean it?"

"I have no alternative," the Marquis answered. "I am blind and, like all women, you will doubtless nag me into doing what you want and it will be quite easy for you because I cannot fight for myself."

"I am quite sure, my Lord, that it would be impossible to make you do anything you did not want to do," Erlina said. "But now that you know what has been happening, I feel equally sure that you will want to make the village a living community once again."

"Now you are trying the feminine approach," the Marquis remarked.

Erlina felt almost as if he had hit her,

She rose from the chair where she had been sitting.

The Marquis put out his hand to stay her.

"Forgive me and don't go away," he asked, "I have been in a fiendish bad humour since I had this accident and was told I had to remain blindfolded for perhaps months until my eyes healed."

He paused for a moment and then added,

"I thought at first I would stay in London and be entertained by the amusing people I call my friends."

"Why did you not do so?" Erlina asked.

"Because I found almost at once that people never behave quite normally to a man who is blind. They say soothing and ingratiating things to you as if they were talking to an idiot and it appeared to me that many of them raised their voices, as if they thought that I was deaf as well as blind."

Erlina then sat down again.

"Now you will understand what I was saying to you just now," she said. "To get well again you have to use your brain and your perception – and that is what is already beginning to work."

The Marquis did not speak, but he was listening to her as she went on,

"Because you cannot see, other parts of your anatomy are beginning to work. You are aware when people are placating you, which is something that you very likely would not have noticed before when you had your sight."

Erlina thought for a moment and then continued,

"I think too that, when people are blind, they are much more attuned to the wonder of the beauty of nature and that is why your instinct told you that you should come to the country."

"Who taught you all this?" the Marquis wanted to know.

"My mother, who was very interested in anything spiritual and had a great knowledge of herbs. We had a Herb Garden at home, which sadly is now overgrown. But I am sure that I can find something that will help to strengthen your eyes and make them heal more quickly if you use it every day."

She paused before she enquired,

"Will you do that?"

"I suppose," the Marquis replied, "if you are going to run my house, you will also have to run me and I shall have to do what you tell me."

"That is certainly a step in the right direction," Erlina smiled.

Then she laughed.

"Why are you laughing?" the Marquis asked.

"Because I cannot believe this is happening," she replied. "I have hated and hated you! I prayed to God, although I tried not to, that He would punish you for what I thought was your cruelty and your wickedness."

"And He has done so very efficiently," the Marquis murmured sharply.

"That may have been a punishment," Erlina said. "At the same time it has brought you home and given you a chance to redeem yourself by helping those who are still here."

"And you are just waiting to give me a list of them!" the Marquis suggested.

"Of course!" Erlina agreed in a different tone of voice. "We can start with the Vicar and then Mr. Cranley."

"Before I start bracing myself for another lecture," the Marquis said, "I would appreciate something to drink and perhaps a good luncheon."

Erlina laughed.

"And where do you think it is to come from?"

"You will find that I have brought a case of champagne down with me in case the cellar has run dry over the years," the Marquis answered, "but I had not thought of food."

"I will now go and see if there is anything available that Mrs. Dawes can cook for you," Erlina said, "and, as you have brought grooms here with you, it would be sensible if we could send one to the next village to buy some provisions."

The Marquis made a gesture with his hands.

"That comes under your department, Miss Sherwood."

Erlina's heart gave a little leap.

Then she said,

"Do you mean – that I can order – anything I want, my Lord?"

"Of course," the Marquis agreed, "and I may tell you that I am very particular as to what I eat and I naturally expect only the best."

"Now I know I am dreaming!" Erlina cried. "I can only hope that I don't wake up too quickly!"

She then ran from the room while she was still speaking.

She crossed the hall towards a long corridor that she was sure would lead to the kitchens.

As she did so, she thought that she heard the Marquis laughing.

CHAPTER THREE

Erlina ran down the corridor to what she thought looked like the kitchen door.

When she opened it, she saw to her astonishment that there were five men as well as Mr. and Mrs. Dawes seated at the kitchen table.

Gerry was there too, eating a large sandwich with some relish.

For a moment the men stared at her before they rose to their feet.

She then walked towards them.

"I expect Dawes will already have told you," she said, "that I am Miss Sherwood. The Marquis has now asked me to run the house for him and I need all your help desperately."

They still stared and next she turned to Dawes and said,

"Dawes, his Lordship wants a glass of champagne at once and you are now engaged as his butler with Mrs. Dawes as his cook."

Mrs. Dawes flung out her arms in delight before she started to cry.

"I thinks we'd die of starvation," she sobbed. "Can what you're a-sayin' really be true?"

"It is true," Erlina said quickly, "but there is no time for you to be crying, Mrs. Dawes, because his

Lordship requires his luncheon as soon as possible."

"And what am I to cook, I'd like to know?" Mrs. Dawes sniffed and then demanded.

She had stopped crying and Erlina saw that she was waiting for an answer.

"We will have to buy some food," she said and held out her hand to the nearest man. "Please tell me who you are."

"I be Jacob the coachman," he answered, "and this 'ere's Sam the footman."

He then indicated the man standing beside him.

Erlina guessed even before the other two men had introduced themselves that they were outriders.

At the end of the table was a man she was sure would be the Marquis's valet.

She was not mistaken.

As she shook his hand, he said,

"I'm Hignet, miss, and I was with his Lordship when he were in the Army."

"Then I shall look especially to you to help me," Erlina said. "We have to cure his eyes and also keep him in a good temper until he can see again."

"That's just what I was thinkin' meself, miss," Hignet agreed.

"So now, what about luncheon?" Erlina asked. "I thought perhaps you, Jacob and Sam, would ride over to the next village and buy everything that Mrs. Dawes needs."

"That'll be everythin' you can think of *and* more," Mrs. Dawes piped up.

"Make a list," Erlina suggested, "and, as those who have come from London with him will know, his Lordship wants only the very best."

Mrs. Dawes gave a little cry of excitement and, opening a kitchen drawer, she looked for a piece of paper to write her requirements down on.

Hignet then intervened in a quiet voice,

"Seein' as how his Lordship ain't been home for six years, miss, I took the liberty of not only bringin' the champagne down with us but also some nice food."

"That is the most wonderful thing I could hear," Erlina exclaimed. "Thank you for being so clever."

She could see that Hignet was really delighted with her praise.

He then explained that among the other things he had brought with him was a superb *pâté* that the chef in London had made with great care and attention before they had departed for Meldon Hall.

There was also a huge uncooked leg of the best lamb and a large cold ham of which they were already eating delicious slices.

When she looked at Dawes, she thought that he appeared spry and even seemed to be a little younger.

It was a long time since they had been able to afford meat unless one counted the few rabbits that he had been able to snare in the Park when no one had been looking.

"Would you be likin' a nice cup of tea, miss?" Mrs. Dawes enquired.

"I would love one," Erlina answered.

Tea, being rather more expensive than the inferior coffee that they had been drinking, was something that she could not afford.

She saw that everybody round the table was drinking tea with the exception of Gerry.

He had a glass of what looked like lemonade and he pushed the last piece of sandwich into his mouth saying,

"That ham was jolly good, Erlina, you should have some to try."

"I will later," Erlina replied. "I have a great deal to catch up with first."

She took Mrs. Dawes to one side of the kitchen and wrote out the long list of what she required.

She knew that Mrs. Dawes could write, but only very laboriously and slowly.

The very considerable list took up both sides of two pieces of paper and, when they had finished, Erlina went back to the kitchen table.

She handed it to the coachman.

Then looking at Hignet she said,

"You must help me. Do we ask his Lordship for money? It might be difficult to open an account so quickly for this long list."

"His Lordship trusts me with his money," Hignet informed her.

He drew from his pocket a large banknote and handed it to Erlina.

She in turn gave it to the coachman and said,

"Please go as quickly as you can and, while you are in the next village, could you please mention that we are looking for staff. We need at least two or three people in the kitchen to help Mrs. Dawes and Dawes will want at least four footmen."

Both Mr. and Mrs. Dawes stared at her as if she was speaking in a foreign language.

Then, as she and Gerry left the kitchen, she heard all of them at once talking at the tops of their voices.

As they reached the hall, Erlina saw the Vicar coming up the steps.

"I suppose Mr. Cranley has been to see you," she asked him.

"He has," the Vicar replied, "and I can hardly believe that, after all these long years, his Lordship has finally returned to his home."

"He is waiting to see you," Erlina told him.

Then she dropped her voice as she went on,

"I don't know if Mr. Cranley told you but his Lordship is temporarily blind."

"Cranley did say that he has suffered an injury to his eyes," the Vicar answered.

"They are closely bandaged and he can – see nothing," Erlina said. "I think you will be surprised at what he has to tell you."

"I have already heard," the Vicar replied.

Erlina walked ahead of him into the sitting room.

"The Vicar is here, my Lord," she said, "and I know that he will be a great help in what is to be a colossal undertaking here at Meldon Hall."

The Vicar walked across the room.

"I am delighted to see you home again, my Lord," he said. "It is a very long time since we have seen each other, but I expect you will remember me?"

"Of course I do," the Marquis answered. "And you have surely been laying a curse on me in the same way that Miss Sherwood has."

"As a Clergyman, I try not to, but instead to seek for an explanation for your Lordship's absence."

"I doubt if you were successful," the Marquis replied dryly. "Now that I am back, I shall need your help."

"You know I am only too willing to give it," the Vicar promised.

"Miss Sherwood has already told me that, like everyone else, you have been very badly treated," the Marquis said. "I must therefore, Vicar, put that right before we start on anybody else."

The Vicar did not speak and the Marquis asked him,

"Tell me what stipend were you receiving when my father was alive?"

"Three hundred pounds a year, my Lord," the Vicar replied, "but, of course, it ceased on your father's death."

"Then why, considering that you were not paid, did you not leave Meldon?" the Marquis asked.

"The people I had looked after for a number of years needed me," the Vicar said simply. "Even when they were dying from cold and starvation they wanted me to be there and I could not abandon them."

Erlina, listening, knew that the Marquis could not fail to be aware of his sincerity.

There was silence until the Marquis sighed,

"I am very grateful to you, which is something I had never expected to say in Meldon. In future you will receive five hundred pounds a year and just as soon as Cranley returns he will make you out a Note of Hand for what you are owed for the five years since my father's death and that will amount to no less than two thousand, five hundred pounds."

For a moment the Vicar could not speak.

Then he said in a somewhat unsteady voice,

"Did – did you say – two thousand, five hundred pounds – my Lord?"

"I think that would be fair and, as soon as you find me the largest and most reliable firm of builders to repair the cottages in the village, we shall at once start on the Vicarage."

"I think I am dreaming!" the Vicar murmured.

Erlina laughed.

"That is what I have been thinking ever since I found his Lordship when I came here."

"Things are already being put in their right places," the Marquis said sharply, "but we have to face reality. Cranley has doubtless told you that I sent him to find servants to staff the house. Is it possible to persuade people to come back to the village or new people to settle here?"

"I have kept in touch with some of those who have left," the Vicar said, "and I think a fair number of them would be happy to return to Meldon if the village is restored to what it was when they lived here. Others, however, may be feeling too bitter to do so."

"Then the first thing we must do is to make the place habitable," the Marquis insisted, "and to see that my own roof does not collapse on my head."

The Vicar looked at Erlina.

"It will be a big job," he cautioned.

"However big, I want it done immediately," the Marquis asserted. "I may be blind, but I have no wish to be uncomfortable as well."

"I am sure that Erlina will do everything in her power to prevent you from suffering any more than can be avoided," the Vicar said quietly, "and, if you can put back the clock, then I am sure that a great number of people, including myself, will bless you for doing so."

"That is much better than bearing the burden of your curses!" the Marquis said a little cynically. "Which I am sure that Miss Sherwood thinks is a direct punishment from Heaven for the way I have behaved."

"If we are going to turn over a new leaf and get you well," Erlina said, "you will have to forget the past and think only of the future."

The Vicar smiled at her.

"You are quite right, but his Lordship must appreciate that it will be a Herculean task not only to re-build the village but also to restore the land that has been allowed to run wild for these past five years."

"I want competent men who know their job," the Marquis said, "and they will work not only on Meldon soil but also on Miss Sherwood's estate next to mine."

"That is not as important as yours, my Lord," Erlina pointed out quickly.

"Not so, they are equally important," the Marquis contradicted her, "and it is part of the price I am prepared to pay for your services."

Erlina gave a little laugh and then turned to the Vicar,

"When I came to you in despair last night, I never imagined that today I would not only have somewhere to live with Gerry but also be offered a very difficult but fascinating job. His Lordship, as you will realise, is employing me and Mr. and Mrs. Dawes, who are ecstatic at knowing that they can have a decent square meal again after so long."

Even as she spoke, Dawes came in carrying a silver tray that clearly wanted cleaning and on it was a bottle of champagne and a number of glasses.

He had, Erlina noticed at once, brushed his hair and straightened his necktie and in fact he looked quite respectable as he came across the room and set down the tray on a small table by the fireplace.

"Shall I pour out the champagne, my Lord?" he asked in a respectful voice.

"Yes, of course," the Marquis answered, "and I am delighted that you and your wife are here to work for me."

"We're very very grateful to your Lordship for having us," Dawes replied.

He poured out the champagne and then he handed first a glass to Erlina, then one to the Marquis and one to the Vicar.

"Can I have some champagne," Gerry asked. "I have never tasted it."

"You can have a sip of mine," Erlina answered with a smile.

She handed him her glass and Gerry took a cautious sip.

"It's not bad," he said, "but I think I like lemonade better."

"That is very sensible of you," the Marquis said. "You stick to lemonade until you are my age."

"I have been to see your horses again," Gerry answered, "and they are more comfortable than they were when they first arrived. But now two of them have to go shopping."

The Marquis smiled.

"That will be a new experience for them and tomorrow, if they are not tired, you must ride whichever one you fancy."

"Thank you, *thank you*!" Gerry cried. "I will just go to see which ones they are taking shopping."

He ran from the room and Erlina said,

"There is no doubt as to who will be the happiest person in Meldon now that you have returned. Gerry has always been obsessed with horses, like his father. But we had only three rather old ones. I was just wondering, my Lord, if you would allow me to bring the two that are left at Sherwood House into your stables?"

"Of course you must bring them here," the Marquis replied. "Send my outriders over immediately to fetch them. They can lead them back."

"I think what I will do, if you will allow me," Erlina said, "is to send Gerry with them to show them the way and he can ride one of the horses back."

"That is a good idea," the Vicar chimed in. "Gerry is a good rider and your Lordship can trust him."

"I am trusting both you and Miss Sherwood to carry out my instructions," the Marquis said, "and that is to get busy right away. I want everything done as quickly as possible."

"We can but try," the Vicar said. "I have never been given a task which is nearer to my heart and I am exceedingly grateful for it, both to your Lordship and, of course, to God."

"If you and Miss Sherwood preach at me for much longer," the Marquis insisted, "I shall really believe it is God who has visited my blindness upon me, not only to punish me for my sins but also to make quite certain that I make reparations for them."

"That appears to me to be a reasonable view, my Lord," the Vicar concurred.

He spoke with a note of amusement in his voice.

For a moment Erlina held her breath just in case the Marquis thought that they had been insulting.

Instead of which he chuckled.

"I have always been suspicious of people who twist the Bible to make it say what they want it to say."

"I think that is forgivable if they need something very badly," the Vicar replied.

Because Dawes had left the room, Erlina refilled the Marquis's glass from the bottle of champagne and then the Vicar's.

"If you will look after his Lordship for a few minutes," she said to the Vicar, "I am going upstairs to see what the condition is of the rooms on the first floor."

"By all means do," the Vicar replied, "I hope that at least some of them are undamaged, but, of course, the beds will need proper airing."

"That is just what I was thinking," Erlina answered.

She went from the room as the Vicar sat down beside the Marquis.

Outside in the hall she found Hignet.

"I am just going up to look at the bedrooms," she told him. "Will you come with me to see if his Lordship's at any rate is habitable?"

"That's just what I were about to do, miss," Hignet replied. "This be a fine house if it wasn't for the dust and dirt of ages."

"Mr. Cranley has done his best to keep it habitable," Erlina said, "but as you can imagine for one man by himself it was a hopeless task."

They walked up what was a magnificent staircase to the first floor.

The State rooms opened off a wide corridor.

The first two or three bedrooms they looked at seemed to be just liveable in, if very dusty with cobwebs everywhere. In another bedroom some birds had somehow crept in and built nests on the cornices below the ceilings.

In two other rooms the ceilings had fallen down, making a mess over what Erlina knew were classical *Aubusson* carpets.

To her delight, however, the Master Suite was in reasably good condition.

It was, of course, thick with layers of dust and the fireplace had not been cleared of ashes since it was last used.

But the huge four-poster bed with its carved posts and brightly gilded canopy had not been affected by the passing years.

The velvet curtains needed shaking, but the Marquis's Coat of Arms embroidered above the headboard was undamaged.

"We need hot bedpans to air the mattresses," Erlina said. "I am sure that there must be plenty of them somewhere in the house."

She was not to be disappointed.

There were a number of them hanging on the wall of the housemaids' cupboards.

She then saw with some delight that the linen cupboard, which still smelt of lavender, was filled with clean sheets and pillowcases.

"It says a great deal for the people in the village," Erlina said, "that none of these things have been stolen while the house has been empty with only one man to guard it."

"I were just thinkin' that," Hignet agreed, "but from what I hears from Mr. Dawes, they be too weak to walk up the drive and far too hungry to want anythin' but food."

"That is indeed true," Erlina said in a low voice, "and I am afraid that, however much his Lordship tries to put things right, these last few years will never be forgotten."

"Now don't you go thinkin' like that miss," Hignet said. "We was often hungry, cold and miserable in Portugal in the Peninsular War but when 'twere all over and we'd won the Battle of Waterloo, we'd all but forgotten the bad times and only thinks of the good."

"I hope you are right," she replied, "and one day I hope you will tell me about the Battle of Waterloo."

"His Lordship be brave as a lion," Hignet said, "and when the Duke of Wellington gives him a medal for gallantry, he says that no one deserved it more than he did."

Erlina thought that this was something she had never expected to hear about the Marquis yet even if she had, it was doubtful if she would have thought any better of him.

They went through a number of other rooms and Erlina decided that it was best for her and Gerry to be on the second floor until the roof was repaired.

She also insisted that the coachman and footmen and the two outriders with, of course, Hignet, should be on the first floor of the South wing.

"It would be a great mistake," she explained, "for anyone to go higher until the roof is properly repaired. I saw how quickly our own roof collapsed in the fire. I don't want to take the risk of anyone sleeping under this one until we know that it is really safe."

"That be kind of you, miss, and I agrees with every word you say," Hignet replied.

It took them some time, because the house was so big, to inspect just the first floor in the centre block.

When she finally went down the stairs again, Erlina found that the Vicar had gone home and the Marquis was alone.

She told him what they had been doing and he listened to her attentively.

Then she added a little nervously,

"You must tell me exactly what – you want to do. The first thing is whether you wish to have luncheon in the dining room and I assume that – you would prefer to be alone."

The Marquis was silent for a moment.

Then he said,

"Yesterday I should most certainly have said 'alone', as I did not want anybody to see me making a fool of myself while eating. But today we have so much to discuss and I have so much to hear about my possessions, that you and Gerry will eat with me."

"You are – quite sure that you – want us?" Erlina asked a little nervously.

"I want you," the Marquis confirmed, "and, as you are looking after me, you can cut up my food, which Hignet has been doing for me."

"I shall like being with you," Erlina said without thinking.

"That is certainly an admission in the right direction," the Marquis responded mockingly.

"You were very kind to the Vicar," Erlina went on, "and I am more than grateful."

"Did it matter so much to you?" the Marquis enquired unexpectedly.

"Of course it did," she replied. "He is a part of my life, just as the people in the village have been a part of my life from the time I was a child."

She paused for a moment before she added,

"Perhaps you don't understand because you have been in the War and travelled and have lived in London. But I have lived only here. Unless you invite people to stay and talk to you, I am afraid you are going to find my conversation very dull and repetitive."

There was a short silence before the Marquis said,

"I am using my perception, as you told me to do and, although you may have lived only in one place physically, I think you have travelled to many parts of the world in your mind."

Erlina clapped her hands.

"That is very clever of you and exactly how I want you to think. I am sure that when you were talking to the Vicar you realised what a good and sincere man he is."

"I thought while you were listening that it was what you thought I should be thinking," the Marquis said.

Erlina laughed.

"You are the best pupil I have ever had. If you go on like this, I shall soon be learning from you rather than you learning from me."

"Perhaps we have a great deal to teach each other," the Marquis suggested,

There was a little pause before he added,

"I think that you and I should make a pact, Erlina, I am becoming bored with calling you 'Miss Sherwood' and that is to be honest with each other."

"But, of course," Erlina agreed.

"You have been honest in telling me how much you have hated me and I have confessed to you the reason for my behaviour," the Marquis went on. "I do have a feeling, although I may be wrong, that there will be a great many problems in the future that we will have to share if we are to put things right here."

He paused a moment and then went on,

"I want you to stop being afraid of me and always tell me the truth."

"I promise, I promise," Erlina answered, "and talking to you will be exactly like talking to Papa – before he fell ill. He was so clever and had seen so much of the world that he made me see it through his eyes."

She paused and then added a little shyly,

"I am thinking that – perhaps for the moment you – could use my eyes."

"That is what I want to do," the Marquis answered, "but you do promise you will always tell me the truth?"

He put out his hand as he spoke and Erlina put her hand into it.

"I promise," she said very softly.

*

Luncheon was late, but when it came Erlina, who by this time was very hungry, thought that it was the most delicious meal that she had ever eaten.

They had sat in the beautiful dining room that had been designed and built by the famous Robert Adam. It had alcoves in which stood statues of the Gods and Goddesses of Ancient Greece.

The walls were painted in the special green that was the Adams's particular colour and the ceiling was exceptionally fine as was the pretty marble fireplace that wanted cleaning, as did the windows and the sideboards.

But Dawes had managed to remove all the dust off the polished table.

Erlina thought that with a few more cleanings it would look as it had at the beginning of the century when the Prince of Wales, as he then was, had made it fashionable not to use a tablecloth.

The Marquis sat at the top of the table with Erlina on his right and Gerry on his left.

Dawes, looking more like himself than he had for many years, handed round the dishes that had been brought from the kitchen.

They were placed on the sideboard by Hignet and one of the outriders.

They started with the *pâté* that Hignet had brought down from London.

Then came the large leg of lamb that had been excellently roasted by Mrs. Dawes and someone must have found some vegetables in the Kitchen Garden, which was close by the stables.

There were even a few very new small potatoes, which might have been dug up quickly and as he knew that that they were hungry, Dawes gave both Erlina and Gerry extra-large helpings.

She doubted if she would get through it all as she cut up some thin slices of lamb for the Marquis.

He managed to eat it very elegantly, she noticed, without dropping anything on the table or down his clothes.

She was certain that he was very fastidious and she could understand the reason why at first he wanted to eat by himself and not have anybody watching him.

To make the Marquis feel at ease she talked not about the village or the sufferings of the people.

Instead she discussed the places in the world that her father had visited.

Then she told him of her mother's interest in special herbs that promoted healing.

"I think some people thought that Mama was a White Witch," she related, "but they all came to her. And, as the only doctor in the vicinity was several miles away, no one sent for him unless they were dying or had broken an arm or a leg."

"And so you have carried on where your mother left off," the Marquis suggested.

"I am not nearly as knowledgeable as Mama was," Erlina replied, "but I try to remember exactly what she told me. While Gerry and I were trying to keep the house clean, we used also to do some weeding in the Herb Garden."

She could not help thinking that this sort of conversation must bore the Marquis.

He was used to the wit and chatter of the smartest people in London Society.

Hignet brought in the last course. It was cheese that he had brought down from London.

When he had left the room, Erlina turned to the Marquis,

"Now it is your turn to tell me about the places you have been to and the things you have done. And both Gerry and I are longing to hear about the Battle of Waterloo and the medal you won for bravery."

"I suppose Hignet has been talking to you," the Marquis said. "He makes so much fuss about that medal that he might easily have won it himself!"

"I am sure he deserved one," Erlina said, "and he has been so helpful already that I am prepared to award him a dozen medals if he goes on the way he has started."

"I want to hear about the Battle of Waterloo," Gerry insisted.

He had not said very much during the meal and now after he had drunk a little lemonade, he wiped his mouth and looked expectantly at the Marquis.

For a moment Erlina thought that he would refuse to discuss the battle.

Then, as if he did not wish to disappoint Gerry, he started to tell him what he wanted to know.

How the Prussian Guards had come to the rescue just at the right moment for the British Forces who were outnumbered.

How, almost at the last minute, the tide had turned and Napoleon had been defeated and there were tremendous casualties on both sides.

Gerry listened wide-eyed and the Marquis finished by saying,

"When I am able to see again, I will draw you a map so that you can see exactly how the Regiments were lined up against each other on that fateful day."

"I would like that," Gerry replied excitedly.

"But make no mistake, Gerry," the Marquis went on with his story, "war is wrong, cruel and very unpleasant. There are moments of elation when a battle has been won, but victory demands a terrible price in human suffering and loss of life."

"I did not think about that," Gerry replied.

"Then think about it now," the Marquis answered, "and while you love horses, you must be aware that hundreds of horses died or were wounded in battle. Their screams when they were hit by a cannonball is something I can never forget."

He spoke very earnestly and with conviction.

Again Erlina thought that he was very different from what she had expected of the man she had hated for so long and had prayed would suffer.

Unexpectedly she now found herself saying a different prayer.

She thought that, if it surprised her, it would, if he was aware of it, certainly surprise the Marquis.

'Please, God,' she found herself whispering in her heart, 'let him be – able to see again.'

CHAPTER FOUR

Erlina burst into the drawing room where the Marquis was sitting and exclaimed,

"I have found it! *I have found it!*"

"What have you found?" the Marquis asked.

"The fennel and eyebright for your eyes."

"In your Herb Garden, I suppose," the Marquis remarked.

"Yes, and it was easy to find the fennel, but very difficult to find the eyebright because it is so small."

"I don't suppose they will do me any good," the Marquis commented rather ungratefully.

Erlina drew in her breath.

"You are not very encouraging, my Lord," she said, "and it took me a long time to – find them."

The way she spoke sounded tragic and unexpectedly the Marquis held out his hand.

"Come here," he said.

Reluctantly she moved a little closer to him, then, as his hand was still outstretched, put hers into it.

"I think," the Marquis said quietly, "it upset you going back and seeing what was left of your house."

Erlina's fingers tightened on his.

Then she answered in a broken little voice,

"It – was terrible – awful, there are just – a few bits of the walls – standing and ashes that are still – smouldering."

As if she could not bear the thought of it any more, she sank down on her knees beside the Marquis, taking her hand away from his.

"What will – become of – Gerry and me?" she asked. "What – shall we do? Where – can we possibly go?"

There was a frantic note in her voice.

"I thought you were happy here," the Marquis stated.

"We are – of course, we are," Erlina said. "But we – cannot stay for – ever. Sometime – you will get – married and then – "

"I shall never marry," the Marquis remarked sharply.

The way he spoke was so surprising that Erlina looked up at him, her eyes wide in her pale face.

"Never – marry?" she repeated. "But – why not?"

There was a pause as if the Marquis was reluctant to answer her question.

Then he said,

"One cannot trust a beautiful woman not to behave as my mother did in not being at all interested in her husband or, for that matter, in me."

Erlina sat back on her heels.

"You may have thought like that in the – past," she said, "but now you are – different. You have learnt not to look with your eyes – but with your – heart."

The Marquis did not answer, but she knew that he was listening to her intently and she went on,

"How do you think you – knew just now that I was very upset – at seeing my home? You could not see me and I was – determined as I came back that you should – not know I had been so upset."

"All right," the Marquis said, "I agree that I do use my instinct more than I used to when I could look at people and believe what they told me without realising it that was all lies."

"That is at – least an advance," Erlina answered, "and I have – something else I – want to suggest to you."

"What is it?"

She hesitated before she replied,

"When I was – searching for the herbs – which I know will help you – I felt sure that – Mama was beside me."

She looked at him quickly as if she expected him to say something cynical or at least to show it on his face.

She was, however, reassured and she went on,

"When I found them – I felt that Mama was – telling me I must – try to heal your eyes as – she healed people in which she was always successful."

Again Erlina waited as if she expected the Marquis to say that it was all nonsense and he was not having any part of it.

Instead he said,

"What do you wish to do?"

"I would like to put my hands over your eyes and pray, as Mama did. But you will have to co-operate in a way which I will explain to you when we do it, my Lord."

There was a short silence.

"Very well," the Marquis replied. "I agree. In fact I will agree to anything that will make me see again."

"You will see – you will – I know it!" Erlina cried.

She rose from the floor.

"I am going to change now," she said, "into one of the lovely gowns I found stored in the attic and I hope, even though you cannot see me, you will realise that I am looking extremely smart, in fact, very unlike myself."

"Now you are speaking exactly like a woman," the Marquis teased her.

Erlina did not answer.

She was feeling so delighted that he had agreed to let her try to heal his eyes that she ran as quickly as she could to her bedroom.

Yesterday she and Gerry had explored the attics while the Marquis was busy talking to a man whom Mr. Cranley had brought to the house.

He was a farmer who had lost his farm during the War and was longing to get back to the soil.

Erlina and Gerry had gone up to the attic and found that while rain had come through in some places, the roofs of the North and South wings were undamaged and still sturdy.

In the North wing there were a number of leather trunks.

When Erlina opened them, she found that they contained the clothes that had belonged to the Marquis's mother and had been brought from London to Meldon Hall when she died.

There were six of them filled with pretty gowns, cloaks, furs and lingerie.

All of the most exquisite and expensive kind.

There was also in the attic the clothes that the Marquis had worn when he was a boy.

They had been carefully packed away by the housekeeper as he had grew out of them.

Some of them fitted Gerry perfectly when he tried them on.

He had run downstairs to tell the Marquis as soon as he was free what they had found.

He had agreed to Gerry keeping anything that he might require and gave Erlina the same permission.

"Do you really mean that I can wear those beautiful gowns?" she asked him.

"It would be a great pity to leave them in the attics to rot," the Marquis pointed out.

"It will save me from worrying about my appearance and having to ask you for money in advance, my Lord."

"Of course. You have only one gown!" the Marquis expostulated. "I should have thought of that myself."

"I have had it for three years and it is not only threadbare but beginning to split at the seams," Erlina confessed.

"The wardrobes in the attic are yours as far as I am concerned," the Marquis said, "and we must ask Cranley to find somebody who can alter the dresses that are too big for you."

"How do you know I am not bigger and perhaps fatter than your mother?" Erlina asked.

"I have been working it out for myself," the Marquis answered. "I know that your head is level with my shoulders. I know too that you have been eating very little for some time, so you must be thin. And you are also very light on your feet."

Erlina clapped her hands together.

"That is clever of you!" she enthused. "And, of course, you are right."

Now when she was putting on one of the beautiful gowns, which had come from Bond

Street, she wished that the Marquis could see her in it and perhaps admire her.

Then she told herself sharply that it was something that he was very unlikely to do and he was obviously used to being surrounded by the best dressed and most beautiful women in London.

And she was only a country bumpkin.

As she walked down the stairs, she thought over what the Marquis had said about never wanting to be married.

She knew that it was wrong for him to be thinking like that.

Of course he must be married because he must have a son to inherit the title and to live in splendour at Meldon Hall.

'Once he has restored it and the estate is working at full capacity,' she told herself, 'I feel sure that he will want not one son but several to enjoy it as much as he will.'

It suddenly struck her that maybe he would want to go back to London and in which case once again the place might become as run down as it was now.

'He must not do that – he *must* not,' she told herself firmly.

She then wondered how she could encourage him to make it one of the most outstanding estates in the whole country.

As she reached the hall, Dawes came from the direction of the pantry.

"Luncheon's ready to be served, Miss Erlina," he announced, "and the Missus'll be ever so upset if what she's cooked doesn't please his Lordship."

"How have the girls been?" Erlina enquired.

The Vicar, by what seemed to be a veritable miracle, had produced the two daughters of one of the families who had been obliged to leave the village.

They had been willing to come back to work at The Hall.

Erlina thought that their food should take priority over the cleaning of the house and she had therefore given both the girls to Mrs. Dawes to assist her in the kitchen.

Once they had arrived Mrs. Dawes had become a different person.

She looked younger, she laughed all the time, talked incessantly and was producing the most delicious meals that any of them had tasted for years.

Dawes now had one footman, a rather stupid boy, but at least he was a pair of hands.

The Vicar, on his last visit, had said that he was on the track of another footman.

'What we want now is housemaids,' Erlina thought as she walked into the room where the Marquis was sitting.

He was talking to Gerry, who had just come from the stables where he had spent most of his time with the horses.

"Luncheon is now ready," Erlina said, "and, if we are not hungry, Mrs. Dawes will be very disappointed."

"I am very hungry," Gerry replied, "and Mrs. Dawes's food is scrumptious. I shall soon be so fat that I shall need a bigger pair of breeches from the store upstairs!"

"They are waiting for you whenever you require them," Erlina replied, "and I hope you remembered to thank his Lordship for letting you have them."

"I thanked him – I did thank you, my Lord, did I not?" Gerry said to the Marquis.

"Of course you did," the Marquis agreed, "and I hope you look as smart in them as I did when I wore them all those years ago."

He had risen from his chair and put his hand on Gerry's shoulder.

The boy guided him across the room and through the door into the hall.

Walking behind them both, Erlina thought how tall and strong the Marquis looked with his broad shoulders.

As Gerry chatted away happily, she told herself again that, of course, he must have a son and it would be foolish of him to let his unhappy childhood go on hurting him.

They reached the dining room.

Dawes and the footman had now made it spotlessly clean and the table was shining like a mirror.

They sat down as they always did with the Marquis between them.

Gerry went on talking excitedly about the horses and some of the things he had found in the attic.

"Did you know, my Lord, that there is a bow and arrow up there," he asked, "and several duelling pistols."

"You might try shooting with the bow and arrows," the Marquis replied, "but I think you must get a little older before you start duelling!"

"Have you ever fought in a duel?" Erlina then asked him.

"Yes," the Marquis answered, "and I am delighted to say that I came out the winner."

Erlina was just about to ask him what was the reason for the contest.

Then she thought she could guess that it had involved a woman and it would have been a question of who owned her at the end of the duel.

She could understand that the Marquis was delighted that he had won, but at the same time she could not help wondering herself what this woman had looked like and if she was very lovely.

Perhaps the Marquis had been very happy with her. Then she told herself that was all in the past and anyway it would be a great mistake to question him about his private life.

When luncheon was finished, Gerry went off to the stables again and the Marquis said to Erlina,

"Now, what are we going to do?"

'You know – what I want to do," she answered.

"Very well. I am in your hands. Where shall we go?"

"I want to take you to the Music Room," Erlina replied. "I only discovered it yesterday and besides being a really beautiful room with windows that open onto the garden, it actually contains a very fine piano."

She started to lead the Marquis down the corridor.

"Now I think about it," he said, "just before my mother died, I remember her buying a Broadwood Grand. I suppose it must have been for here rather than for London."

"It is a Broadwood that I found," Erlina said, "and it is very thrilling as it is one with the iron tension bars, which not many people have yet seen."

"Are you telling me in some obscure way," the Marquis wanted to know, "that you play the piano?"

"But, of course, I do," Erlina replied, "but whether you will enjoy what I play is quite a different matter."

"I think I should warn you that I am very critical," the Marquis said teasingly.

"That is what I would expect," she re-joined.

They reached the Music Room and Erlina glanced at the piano, which was standing on a dais.

It was, she thought, the most precious thing in the room and a treasure that she would love to own herself.

However for the moment she recognised that she had to think only about the Marquis.

She led him to the long French windows, which opened out onto the garden.

By now the sun was swelteringly hot, but there was still a faint breeze blowing over the neglected lawns and flowerbeds, which had run wild without care and love.

Erlina had told Dawes what she intended to do and he had lowered the sun-blind over the windows. It was faded and torn at the edges, but it could still keep the sun from entering the Music Room.

There was a comfortable armchair facing the window and Erlina then led the Marquis to it,

As she said,

"Your chair is right in front of you. When you sit down, you will feel the cool air coming through the trees and smell the few flowers that are just outside."

She paused a moment to think and then continued,

"I expect you remember the Rose Garden with the sundial in the centre of it, which I am sure is very old."

The Marquis did not answer, but lowered himself carefully into the chair.

When he stretched out his legs, Erlina brought a low stool and placed it under his feet.

"What happens now?" he asked.

She thought that there was a slightly hostile note in his voice as if he resented being so helpless.

"Now you have to help me," Erlina said softly, "and you must remember that, while my mother taught me what to do, I have never done this before without her being present to help me in case I said something wrong."

The Marquis did not reply and she went on,

"I want you to relax and to think that you are seeing a light, a vivid light, pouring down upon you and especially penetrating your eyes. Do not think of anything else, just the light coming from the sky."

As she spoke, she moved behind the Marquis's chair.

Bending forward she next put her hands very gently over the black bandage that covered his eyes.

She could feel his skin under her little finger and thumb of each hand. Her other fingers rested on the bandage.

Then she prayed, as her mother had taught her, that the Life Force would pour through her hands and bring the Marquis back his sight.

She did not know how long she prayed for.

She felt as if she poured her whole being towards him.

She then gave him the Life Force from herself as well as from the dazzling light that she believed he was receiving from Heaven.

She took her hands from his eyes and without speaking walked slowly towards the piano and sat down on the stool.

She thought at this moment that there was no music she knew that was appropriate for what she was feeling and what she hoped the Marquis felt too.

Instead she played as she had often improvised to herself.

It was the music of the woods, the flowers, the little birds singing in the trees and the fish swimming in the clear stream.

Only after she had played for perhaps twenty minutes did she feel as if she had become herself again.

She was no longer being carried away as she had been while she was trying to heal the Marquis.

She stopped playing and was still for a moment with her hands resting in her lap.

Then she rose and walked to his chair.

She thought at first that he had fallen asleep, but, as she stood looking down at him, the Marquis said,

"Thank you, Erlina! I feel sure that your prayers, if nothing else, have helped me."

"Do you – mean – that? Do you – really mean – it?"

"I would not tell you anything but the truth," he replied. "The truth is that, while I knew that you were praying for me and while I tried to see the light you told me to look for, I did not know, how could I know, whether if my eyes were unbandaged, I would see any more than I could before you tried to heal me."

"You cannot expect miracles the first time I try," Erlina answered, "and I want – you to let me try again."

"You may try as often as you like," the Marquis said, "and I enjoyed the way you were telling me what is happening in my woods, my gardens and my stream."

Erlina stared at him.

Then she gave a little cry.

"How did you know I was telling you that?"

"I knew that was what you were playing on the piano."

"Now you are – really beginning to look with your heart," Erlina said. "Do you think you would have known what I was saying to you in prayer a month ago?"

"I suppose you are right," the Marquis said ruefully, "and I am using my perception in a way I have not used it before."

"Of course you are," Erlina smiled, "and, please, may I ask you if I can do something else?"

"What is that?" the Marquis enquired.

"Can I – when you are in the dark, try to heal your eyes when you are not – wearing your – bandages?"

For a moment she thought that the Marquis was going to refuse and then he said,

"All right. You can come to my room when I am ready for bed and Hignet removes my bandage. Do you really think it will make any difference if you actually touch my eyes?"

"Yes I do," Erlina declared, "and thank you, thank you. I know that what I am trying to do will be more effective if I can actually feel your eyes with my fingers."

She stood for a moment feeling emotional at the thought.

Then she walked out through the window onto the terrace that bordered the Rose Garden.

"Why have you left me?" the Marquis asked.

"I am just thinking," Erlina replied, "that very soon you will be able to see how beautiful the roses are despite having had no attention and the lawn wants cutting but it is still very green."

"We must employ some gardeners," the Marquis suggested sharply.

The way he spoke awoke Erlina from the dream that she had moved in ever since she had prayed for the Marquis.

She turned back.

"Yes, of course we must," she agreed. "But housing must have priority and, as you told the workmen to restore the Vicarage first, they have only just started on one of the cottages."

"Why can we not employ more men?" the Marquis enquired. "They tell me there is a lot of unemployment and I am certain that men who have been discharged from the Army and Navy can very easily turn their hands to carpentry and painting."

"I know that Mr. Cranley is trying to engage all the Ex-Servicemen he can," Erlina said, "and those I have spoken to who are working on the roof are really thrilled to now be getting employment and to be paid such high wages."

She knew that the Marquis had been very generous in what he had promised those who were starting on the restoration.

But it was difficult for him, Erlina thought, because he could not see to realise how much work there was to be done.

Everything had deteriorated so appallingly in the years when he had totally abandoned his home.

It was wonderful for her to see the Vicar so happy, Mr. Cranley looking a new man and the house gradually losing its dust and dirt.

Some of the windows had been cleaned and the difference between them and those that had not was an incentive to everybody to go on working as hard as they could.

'It is like watching a transformation scene,' Erlina thought to herself.

She had never actually seen one performed, but she had read about them in some of the books that described the Operas that had been staged in Vienna over the years.

She could imagine how exciting and moving it would be, even when one knew only too well that it was all part of an act. But to see it in real life, as she was watching Meldon Hall being restored to its original splendour, was very moving.

"Come and sit down and talk to me," the Marquis commanded. "I am bored with doing nothing and I am thinking that perhaps tomorrow I will go riding."

Erlina gave a cry of horror.

"Of course you cannot do that! It would be far too dangerous. And however careful we were, it would be terrible if you had a fall and did any more damage to your eyes."

"I must have some exercise," the Marquis complained.

"You can exercise yourself morning and evening in your bedroom," Erlina replied, "and, of course, you can walk in the garden and I will be very careful not to allow you to slip or fall down."

"Dammit all!" the Marquis swore fiercely. "I am a man not a puppet!"

Erlina did not speak for a moment and then he said in a contrite voice,

"I do apologise for my language, but it makes me so angry to have to sit here and not be able to do anything. My horses are all in the stables and only Gerry can enjoy himself riding them."

"It is very kind of you to let him do so," Erlina said. "At the same time we have to look after you and protect you."

"That is what I should be saying to you," the Marquis retorted.

"Perhaps you will be able to in a short while," Erlina said soothingly.

She thought as she spoke that, if the Marquis regained his sight, he would probably not want to protect her but somebody very different.

Even as she thought about it, there came the sound of the door of the Music Room being opened.

Then she was aware that two people were walking towards them.

She turned round and stared.

First she saw a tall very fashionably dressed young man of around thirty years old.

With him was a lady who she realised at once was exceedingly beautiful.

She was so arrayed in silk, satin, feathers and diamonds that Erlina felt that she could not be real.

The man walked towards the Marquis and began,

"At last we have found you, Michael! So what in the name of Heaven made you come down here of all places?"

"So it is you, Oliver!" the Marquis remarked. "I cannot think how you managed to find me."

"I just used my brain, my dear cousin," the man called 'Oliver' said, "and when I at last knew where you were, I, of course, came to cheer you up and have brought Isabel with me."

The lady moved forward as the Marquis's cousin spoke and then bent down to kiss him lightly on the cheek.

"I am very angry with you, my dearest, most beloved Michael," she said, "for not telling me where you were going. You know I would have come with you."

"I wanted no one with me," the Marquis replied.

He spoke disagreeably.

His cousin Oliver and the beauty, wearing a white bonnet decorated with flame-coloured ostrich feathers, stared at Erlina.

"And who is this?" Oliver enquired coldly.

"I should have introduced you," the Marquis replied, "to Miss Erlina Sherwood, whose estate marches with this one and who, most unfortunately, has just had her home burnt to the ground."

"That is indeed a disaster," Oliver remarked.

"Erlina," the Marquis went on, "allow me to introduce my cousin, Oliver Mell and Lady Isabel Fisher."

Erlina curtseyed and, while Oliver Mell bowed, she was aware that Lady Isabel looked at her with hostile eyes.

"I cannot imagine," she said softly to the Marquis, "why you did not send for me when you arrived home. After all it is I who should be looking after you and keeping you happy."

"I had no wish to see anyone," the Marquis replied.

"Except, it seems, Miss Sherwood," Lady Isabel murmured.

"Miss Sherwood is helping me to restore the house and the estate to what it was before I neglected it," the Marquis explained.

"Good Heavens!" his Cousin Oliver exclaimed. "You told me you would never set foot in Meldon Hall again! That is why it was the last place I looked for you."

"I changed my mind," the Marquis said shortly. "Until I came here I did not realise what damage I had done by refusing to return home. Now, somewhat belatedly, I am trying to put things to rights."

"Which, of course, is such a wonderful idea of yours," Lady Isabel said, "and you know, dearest Michael, that I will help in every way I possibly can."

She spoke in a cooing seductive voice.

Listening to her, Erlina had the feeling that it somehow did not quite ring true.

She thought too, and she was sure that she was not mistaken, that Oliver Mell was not as fond of his cousin as he was pretending to be.

Feeling somewhat embarrassed by the way they were both looking at her, she said to the Marquis,

"If your guests are staying to tea, my Lord, I will go and arrange for it to be served in the drawing room or would you prefer it here?"

"Staying for tea?" Oliver Mell protested. "We have brought our trunks with us and also our servants. We are going to look after you, Michael, as we would have done if you had not disappeared immediately after your accident."

Erlina saw the Marquis's lips tighten as if he was trying to prevent himself from saying that he did not want them in his house.

Feeling that the situation was becoming somewhat uncomfortable, Erlina walked towards the door.

"I will arrange for tea in the drawing room," she proposed.

As she closed the door behind her, she heard Oliver Mell say,

"Trust you, Michael, to have some beautiful creature around to alleviate your suffering. At the same time is it not a little indiscreet?"

Erlina did not wait to hear the Marquis's reply, but ran down the corridor to the hall.

Dawes was there and she said to him,

"I think we had better have tea in the drawing room please Dawes."

"That's what I thinks you'd want, Miss Erlina," Dawes replied.

As he spoke, Hignet came rushing through the green baize door.

"What's all this?" he asked. "I've just been told that Mr. Oliver's here. And that be bad news!"

"Why do you say that?" Erlina questioned him.

"'Cos them cousins ain't never got on, miss," Hignet replied. "In fact 'twere Mr. Oliver as arranged the Steeplechase when his Lordship were injured."

"They have come to stay," Erlina informed him.

"Not if his Lordship can help it!" Hignet retorted. "He might have to have them here for the night as they've brought a whole crowd with them."

Erlina looked concerned.

"How many?" she asked.

"From what I hears from the men as is workin' in the kitchen, there be a coachman, a footman, two outriders, his valet and her Ladyship's maid besides two men on the brake."

Erlina put up her hands in horror.

"How are we to accommodate so many?" she asked. "Even if they wait on themselves, Mrs. Dawes will not be able to cook for them all."

Hignet thought for a moment.

Then he suggested,

"I thinks, miss, it'd be sensible to say that you'll accommodate Mr. Oliver's valet and her Ladyship's maid for the night, but all the rest'll have to go to the nearest Posting inn. There be one in the next village."

"Yes, I know," Erlina said, "but it seems very inhospitable."

"Don't you worry about that," Hignet said. "Mr. Oliver's been livin' off his Lordship for years! He pleads for money as if he expects it to fall into his hands like manna from Heaven!"

Erlina gave a choked laugh.

Equally she knew that it would be really impossible to have so many people staying in the house when they were not yet ready for lavish parties.

"I don't know how I can tell his Lordship what you suggest," she said at length.

"Leave it to me," Hignet insisted. "He'll know that it's for the best and you can't work miracles."

"Then please tell him that you suggested it," Erlina said, "and I will go and help Mrs. Dawes with the tea."

She went towards the kitchen.

As she did so, she was thinking that the newcomers had swept away all the peace and happiness that she had found since coming to Meldon Hall.

Now she was feeling uncertain of herself and afraid of making mistakes and, most of all, of upsetting the Marquis.

She was very sure in her heart that her healing had done at least some good to his eyes already.

But he could certainly not be upset or worried in any way in his codition.

If, as Hignet had said, he did not get on with his cousin, then Oliver Mell was the last person who she wanted to have at The Hall.

Hignet had said that it was Oliver Mell who was responsible for the Marquis's accident.

If so, he was certainly not welcome here while the Marquis was still blind.

'Oh, why did they have to come?' she asked. 'Why did they have to spoil everything?'

Then she told herself that it was bound to happen sooner or later.

The Marquis might well have tried to escape from the outside world.

But the outside world had come to him.

CHAPTER FIVE

By the time that tea was ready Erlina had helped Mrs. Dawes to produce what was an attractive and delicious meal.

There were sandwiches, scones and hot buttered toast, as well as a number of little cakes and there was a large sultana cake at which Mrs. Dawes was an undoubted expert.

Hignet had helped and then Erlina asked him to go to tell the Marquis and his guests that tea was now ready.

"I hopes that his Lordship's gettin' rid of them, that's what I hopes," Hignet said. "You can bet your last penny as Mr. Oliver'll be schemin' to get some more money out of him and that's a genuine certainty"

"Why should the Marquis be so generous to him?" Erlina asked.

"Mr. Oliver be his Heir Presumptive," Hignet replied.

"Heir Presumptive?" Erlina exclaimed. "Do you mean that – if the Marquis does not have a son, he will inherit the title and the estates as well as the house and all its treasures?"

"That's right, miss," Hignet replied, "and it'd be a disaster, that's what it'd be, a real disaster!"

He walked away towards the Music Room as he spoke and Erlina looked after him with concern in her eyes.

If the Marquis did not have a son, then Oliver Mell would come into the whole estate.

She was certain from what she felt, as well as from what Hignet had told her, that he was a bad man.

Things would then be as bad, if not worse, than they were now.

She knew perceptively that he would not wish to live in the country and would spend all his money and time in London.

'I must persuade the Marquis that he must get married and have a son,' she told herself.

The terrifying question then rose again, what would happen to Gerry and her?

The party came into the drawing room and Lady Isabel looked, Erlina thought, somewhat disdainfully at the food.

She also spoke to Erlina in a hard voice.

It was very different indeed from the cooing dulcet tones that she spoke to the Marquis in.

Erlina had just poured out the tea when Gerry came running into the room.

"What do you think, my Lord," he said to the Marquis before he noticed the newcomers, "there are new horses in the stables, eight of them, but they are not as fine as yours."

He spoke impulsively.

Then he saw that the Marquis was not alone with his sister.

"Who is this, Michael?" Oliver asked him in a suspicious voice. "I did not know you had opened The Hall to children."

The Marquis replied, speaking in the supercilious and cold tone that he had not used for some days.

"Let me introduce you," he said, "to Sir Gerald Sherwood. He is the sixth Baronet and, as I have already told you, he owns the estate that marches with mine."

As Gerry had been well trained by Erlina, he held out his hand first to Lady Isabel and then to Oliver Mell.

"How do you do, sir," he said. "I have been talking to your horses."

"I only wish that they were mine," Oliver Mell replied, "but actually the horses you were disparaging belong to his Lordship."

"They are mine?" the Marquis asked sharply.

"We did not think that Isabel's team was as good as yours, so I borrowed the bays and your carriage to bring her here."

"You did not drive them yourself?" the Marquis enquired.

Oliver Mell gave a somewhat contrived laugh.

"No, Jackson would not let me, so he has come with them, but I have also brought down Titus, the horse you wished to buy from me. I thought it would please you, as you are in the country."

"I would have liked to have seen him first," the Marquis said, "but, as you have brought him with you, I suppose that I must keep my word and give you a thousand pounds for him."

Oliver Mell smiled.

"That is exactly what I require at the moment and I suppose you would not like to make it ten thousand and get me out of the hands of the duns?"

"We have discussed this issue before," the Marquis replied, "and I have not altered my decision."

Oliver Mell shrugged his shoulders and walked away to the window.

Erlina felt that the situation was becoming increasingly uncomfortable and so very bad for the Marquis.

As if she felt the same, Lady Isabel moved to sit down beside him on the sofa.

"You are not to trouble your head over Oliver's difficulties," she told him softly. "I have been so concerned over you, dearest Michael, that it has been impossible to think of anything else."

The Marquis did not reply.

Erlina, having poured out the tea for everyone present, thought that she and Gerry should now leave.

She therefore piled a plate with a number of small sandwiches, cakes and scones and said to Gerry,

"Come with me. There is something I want to talk to you about."

He was eating a sandwich and looked at her in surprise.

Erlina turned to Lady Isabel.

"I am sure, my Lady, you will be kind enough to pour his Lordship another cup of tea if he should want one?"

"You can be quite certain of that," Lady Isabel said tartly, "and kindly see to it that my lady's maid is looked after and my trunks unpacked."

"There is no need to unpack too much," the Marquis interposed. "I am afraid we cannot accommodate you for more than just tonight. The house is not yet ready to receive guests."

Lady Isabel gave a shrill cry.

"Michael! How can you be so unkind when I have come so far just to see you and to help you get well?"

"I need no one's help but Miss Sherwood's," the Marquis replied firmly. "She knows exactly what to do."

"If you propose to send us back tomorrow," Oliver Mell said slowly, turning round from the window, "I think it will be too much of a strain to put on your horses. We came here in a hurry and only spent one night on the road."

The Marquis was silent and Erlina could see that he was frowning.

Then he said,

"Very well, you will stay for two nights and then leave us on Wednesday. It may seem inhospitable but, as I told you, I wish to be alone and the doctors' orders are that I must have complete quiet and on no account should I be upset or stressed."

"Then, of course, dearest Michael," Lady Isabel cooed, "we will do whatever we can to please you. At the same time I cannot imagine how I could upset you in any way."

The Marquis did not reply to this and Erlina walked towards the door.

"I will go and see about the rooms," she then declared, "and talk to Mrs. Dawes about dinner."

Somewhat reluctantly Gerry followed her, but stopped to say to the Marquis,

"The stables are overcrowded and some of the horses, my Lord, will have to go into the paddock."

He did not wait to hear the Marquis's reply, but ran after Erlina.

She took him into the small sitting room on the other side of the hall and gave him the plate that she was carrying.

"We don't want all these people here," Gerry said, "and the coachmen and grooms were all grumbling and saying that there is hardly room 'to swing a cat'!"

Erlina knew that a good part of the stables was uninhabitable and she could understand that the men found it irritating.

She had a great deal to do, however, and left Gerry to go to the kitchen.

Hignet was there and he said as she appeared,

"Now don't you fuss yourself, miss. Everythin's under control and the lot from London's gone off already to the Postin' inn."

Erlina gave a sigh of relief and Hignet went on,

"Except for Jackson. He be one of us, so to speak, so he be stayin' here. I'll find a room for him a bit later."

"The Marquis has told his cousin that they are to leave on Wednesday," Erlina confided.

"That be two nights," Mrs. Dawes said. "There's nobody to make up their beds and do their rooms."

"I have been thinking about that," Erlina added. "Her Ladyship's lady's maid can look after hers and her washing and perhaps Hignet will be kind enough to give me a hand with first cleaning her room and then Mr. Oliver's."

"I just knowed it would be me!" Hignet exclaimed in mock dismay.

But he was smiling and Erlina knew that he would not let her down.

They made rooms ready on the same floor as theirs as Hignet thought that it would be right to use the State rooms.

As Erlina had not been able to engage any housemaids yet, the rooms were very dusty.

All they could do in such a short time was to brush the carpet and dust the dressing table and other furniture.

As they did so, Erlina said to Hignet despairingly,

"How could I have imagined that visitors would arrive before we had time to do anything but clean the downstairs rooms?"

"'Tis always the same," Hignet answered. "Women be just like bees round a honey pot where his Lordship be concerned."

There was a little silence and then Erlina remarked,

"I expect he enjoys that – as any man would."

"They never lasts long," Hignet said, "and if you asks me, her Ladyship be on the way out."

Erlina then thought that it would be incorrect for her to ask him any more questions.

They therefore went from Lady Isabel's room and started to clean what they could of the one that was to be occupied by Oliver Mell.

As she thought about him and what Hignet had said, she felt sure that he would upset the Marquis and therefore the sooner he left the better.

There was, however, nothing that she could do about it.

It was only by a tremendous effort that she had the room at least habitable by the time she had to dress for dinner since Hignet had to leave her to look after the Marquis.

She saw the Marquis coming up the stairs with Hignet and hurried to meet with him as he reached the top.

"I believe, my Lord," she said, "it would be easier if you had dinner alone – with your guests tonight. You will not want Gerry and me with you."

The Marquis had stopped still when she spoke to him and now he said,

"You are in charge of the house, Erlina, and I expect you and your brother to dine with me as you have done so far and I will not have people who drop in unexpectedly upsetting my arrangements."

He sounded as if he was now really annoyed and Erlina felt that it would be a mistake to argue with him.

So she said nothing.

He walked on down the corridor to the Master Suite at the far end of it.

She went into Gerry's room and found him playing with the bow and arrows that he had brought down from the attic.

"The Vicar has put up a target for Tom and me," he then told her. "I shot four bull's eyes today and Tom only got two!"

"That was very satisfactory," Erlina said, "and when we have time we can see if there are some more surprises up there that will amuse you both."

The Vicar had arranged that Gerry and Tom should have their lessons together, starting early next week.

"You cannot expect them not to want to explore everything on the estate first," he said to Erlina, "and they will have to work hard to make up for lost time."

"I think that is sensible," Erlina agreed, "and it would be difficult at the moment to keep them out of the stables."

She had arranged for her brother and Tom to ride every morning and that they were now mounted on the Marquis's fine horses was an inexpressible delight to both of the boys.

She therefore understood when Gerry asked her again,

"Why did those people have to come here? We don't want them."

"They are only staying until Wednesday," Erlina replied, "and you must be very polite to them because they are friends of his Lordship."

"I don't think his Lordship wants them," Gerry commented perceptively.

Erlina thought that she should not contradict or agree with him on this.

Instead she kissed his cheek and suggested,

"We must just make them as comfortable as we possibly can. Now hurry up and change for dinner. And don't forget, go to bed as soon as the meal is finished and without my telling you to do so."

"I will not forget," Gerry nodded, "but I would rather talk to his Lordship than that other man."

Erlina then went to her own room and lay on the bed to think things through.

She could not help being feminine enough to resent Lady Isabel's hostility to her.

She therefore chose to wear for dinner one of the prettiest gowns that she had brought down from the attic.

It was a little too big for her, but fortunately the current fashion had decreed that there should be no waist.

The skirt fell from under the bust. It was decorated with satin flowers round the hem and on the puffed sleeves.

Erlina did not like to think about how much the gown must have cost.

She knew that neither she nor her mother had ever owned such an expensive gown.

It was indeed fortunate that the Marchioness had bought so many clothes shortly before she died.

The fashions too had changed very little in the years after the War, the exception being that gowns had become more elaborate and rather fussy.

She was therefore not surprised when Lady Isabel entered the drawing room wearing a very elaborately decorated gown.

It did not, however, in any way eclipse the one that Erlina was wearing.

She thought that Lady Isabel looked perplexed at her appearance as she snapped sharply,

"I thought from what his Lordship was saying that your house had been burned down."

"It has been," Erlina replied, "but luckily I have something nice to wear tonight."

Lady Isabel looked at her suspiciously.

"Your gown certainly came from Bond Street," she stated, "and you must be very rich to afford one of Madame Rachel's models!"

Erlina did not have to answer her for at that moment the Marquis came into the room.

He had been guided down the stairs by Gerry.

"Oh, here you are, dearest Michael," Lady Isabel gushed.

She walked across the room and kissed him on the cheek.

"It is so lovely to be here with you," she went on.

Then, in what might have been *sotto voce*, but was perfectly audible to Erlina, she asked,

"Surely that child is not dining with us?"

"Gerry is my guest tonight, just as you are," the Marquis said, "and we have dinner early because it suits Mrs. Dawes, my cook."

Watching her, Erlina saw Lady Isabel look at Gerry in the same hostile way as she had at her.

But she was too sensible to say anything.

Oliver Mell came into the room and they moved in to dinner, with Gerry again guiding the Marquis at his request.

Erlina had thought that perhaps the Marquis would not want to eat with so many people present, but she remembered how he had made an exception for having her and Gerry with him when they had first come to The Hall.

It became apparent as the meal progressed that he had arranged everything with Hignet.

The food that was put in front of him had already been cut up and there were no sauces or gravy, which would have made his eating it messy.

Because Erlina thought that she should not push herself forward, she was silent as Lady Isabel talked exclusively to the Marquis.

Oliver Mell was at first silent.

Then, after he had drunk a considerable amount of wine, he became much more voluble.

"Do tell me about yourself, Miss Sherwood," he said, "and why you should waste your beauty on the turnips and cabbages instead of coming to London?"

"The answer to that is quite simple," Erlina replied. "We had little money when the War ended and I had my father's estate to look after."

"Now your house has been burned down, you must come to London, where I prophesy that you will be a great success."

He lowered his voice as he added,

"It cannot be very amusing for you here at Meldon Hall."

"On the contrary, I am very content to help his Lordship restore his house and the village and, of course, to help bring back his sight for him."

"Do you think that is possible?" Oliver Mell asked in a whisper.

"I am quite certain it is," Erlina replied firmly.

She had the feeling that this was not the answer that Oliver Mell was looking for.

She felt, as the dinner progressed, that there was something about him that was distinctly unpleasant.

But she could not explain it even to herself.

But she realised that she was right in thinking that his only motive for seeking his cousin was to extract money from him.

He was also hoping, although she felt that it must be just her imagination, that he would remain blind.

When dinner was over, they all then moved into the drawing room with the gentlemen not remaining behind for a glass of Port.

Erlina thought that she would now retire to her bedroom.

She was just about to say that she would go upstairs with Gerry when the Marquis said,

"I am tired, as I am sure you must be, Isabel, after such a long drive, and I suggest we all go to bed early."

"You are quite right, dearest Michael, as you always are," Lady Isabel answered, "and I am definitely fatigued. I have always disliked the swaying of a carriage down country lanes."

She paused to smile at him before she added,

"And, of course, dearest, there is always tomorrow when we can be together and I have a great deal to say to you."

The Marquis did not answer.

He only rose to his feet and, as if he had ordered him to do so, Gerry went to his side.

The Marquis put his hand on Gerry's shoulder and started to walk towards the door.

Isabel then gave a little cry,

"You did not say 'goodnight' to me unless you would like me to come and see you a little later?"

She said the last few words in a low voice, but Erlina heard them very clearly.

"Certainly not!" the Marquis replied quickly. "I wish to sleep well, Isabel, and I suggest you do the same."

He stopped for a moment and then resumed,

"Goodnight and, if the beds are uncomfortable, it is really your own fault. Naturally we are not yet ready to accommodate visitors and shall not be so for several months yet."

He did not wait for a reply, but went out through the door with Gerry.

Erlina was aware that Lady Isabel was looking at Oliver Mell.

At the same time she made a little gesture with her hands as if she felt that the situation was hopeless.

Leaving them both looking somewhat nonplussed, Erlina hurried after the Marquis and Gerry.

Only as she reached the door did she hear Lady Isabel say,

"Do you think Michael paid for that gown?"

Erlina caught up with the Marquis and they went on slowly up the stairs.

"How have you managed to accommodate them," he asked. "I thought we had no one to help clean the rooms."

"The Vicar has found a housemaid, who is coming next week," Erlina replied, "and Mr. Cranley has heard of one at Boxstead, who he is interviewing tomorrow. In the meantime Hignet and I have done our best."

"I hope to God nobody else finds out where I am," the Marquis said. "I do *not* wish to be seen and I do *not* want to be talked about! All I want is to be left alone."

"Except for us," Gerry piped up. "You do want us, don't you, my Lord?"

There was an anxious note in his voice that was very obvious.

"Of course I want you," the Marquis replied. "Who else would lead me about as well as you do? Who else would take such good care of my horses?"

"I helped the grooms rub down two horses this morning," Gerry boasted, "and they said I did it very well."

"I am sure you did," the Marquis grinned.

They next reached the Master Suite and Erlina saw that Hignet was there waiting for his Master.

"Come on in, my Lord," he said. "What you wants is rest."

"I am sick of resting and I am sick of being blind!" the Marquis exploded.

He spoke petulantly like a child.

"Don't forget that you have the eyebright and fennel to help you," Erlina said. "They are very important."

"I will not forget," the Marquis promised, "and thank you very much, Erlina."

He turned round to put his hand for a moment on her arm.

Then he patted Gerry on the head.

"I have a secret to tell you tomorrow morning," he said.

"A secret!" Gerry exclaimed. "That is very exciting."

"I think that is what you will find it," the Marquis answered.

Hignet led him in through the door and Erlina went with Gerry to his room.

"I wonder what the secret is that he is going to tell me," Gerry looked intrigued.

"If it is a real secret, you must not tell anyone," Erlina replied, "not even Tom, unless the Marquis says you may."

"I hope it's a fabulously scrumptious secret, all for me!"

Erlina helped him undress, heard his prayers and tucked him up in the large bed.

It had been a long day and the boy was obviously very sleepy.

"Goodnight, Erlina," he said as she kissed him. "It is such fun being here!"

"Great fun," she agreed.

She kissed him again, blew out the candle beside his bed and went to the door.

"God and His Angels watch over you, darling," she whispered as she reached it.

She thought, as she went down the corridor, that he was already half-asleep and had not heard her.

She went to her own room and sat down at the French secrétaire that was in a corner of the room.

She began to make a list of all the things that would be required tomorrow.

She knew with the visitors that Mrs. Dawes would want a great deal more provisions from the shops in the next village.

She then decided that it would be best to send one of the outriders early in the morning to collect them.

She then undressed and was just brushing her hair when there came a knock on her door.

She thought that it might be Lady Isabel's lady's maid.

Quickly she pulled on her *negligée* and opened the door.

It was Hignet who stood there.

"If you ain't gone to bed, miss," he said, "his Lordship'd like you to do his eyes."

"Do his eyes?" Erlina repeated in surprise.

"'He said you wanted to do them without a bandage on his face."

"Yes, yes – of course," Erlina answered, "but I did not think that tonight – "

"It's what he wants," Hignet said, "and as you knows, miss, we has to give in to him."

"Y-yes, of course," Erlina agreed.

"He's told me what you said," Hignet went on, "and I've put a chair for him close beside the bed so that when you finish he can get into his bed without any help from you or me."

Erlina nodded to show that she understood his arrangements.

"But if he goes to sleep in it, it won't matter. He'll be comfortable in the chair with his feet up and I've put a blanket over his legs so he won't be cold."

"So you have thought of everything, Hignet," Erlina praised him, "and he is still in the dark?"

"Black as pitch, it be," Hignet said, "and I've took orf his bandage so all you has to do is to go straight to his chair."

"I will come at once," Erlina said.

They walked down the corridor.

"Did his Lordship bathe his eyes?" Erlina asked.

"Before dinner and just now," Hignet answered. "Jest as you says, miss, and there were fennel in with his vegetables."

"That is splendid!" Erlina exclaimed.

The outer door of the Master Suite opened into a small *entresol* where there were two more doors.

One, Erlina knew, led into the bedroom and the other into a boudoir.

"Don't tell his Lordship," Hignet whispered, "or he'll be upset at me molly-coddlin' him, but I be sleepin' on the sofa in there."

He winked as he added,

"I'll stop anybody disturbin' him."

Erlina was still.

It had never struck her that perhaps Lady Isabel might go to the Marquis in the night.

She was very sure that it was something that he did not want at this moment.

Hignet was right in thinking that he would guard him from anyone like a watchful sentry.

They reached the Marquis's door and, when Hignet opened it, Erlina could see a very faint light coming through the slightly open door of the boudoir.

"Miss Sherwood, my Lord," Hignet announced. "I told her where you'd be."

Erlina stepped into the darkness.

She just had a glimpse of the back of a chair.

Hignet then closed the door behind her and now the room was completely dark.

She stood behind the Marquis's chair and said to him softly,

"You know what to do. Think of a light shining down from Heaven and I will then try to make some light pour from me into your eyes."

The Marquis did not answer.

She put out her hands and very gently found his head lying back against a pillow.

He was in exactly the right position for her to put both her hands over both his eyes and the middle fingers of each hand were on the lids themselves.

It gave her a strange feeling to touch his skin.

Yet she knew without him saying anything that he was upset at the arrival of his cousin and Lady Isabel.

He was unable to relax as he had done when she had treated him in the afternoon.

So without explaining why she took her hands from his eyes and started to massage his forehead.

She moved her fingers rhythmically until she felt him respond to their gentleness and he was no longer tense.

She prayed as she moved her fingers up and down on his forehead.

Finally she moved them back onto his eyes.

Now she knew perceptively that he had relaxed and he was thinking of the light shining down from the sky.

She was praying fervently as her mother had taught her to do.

She prayed and prayed, believing that the Life Force was pouring into him through her fingers.

*

A long time later she realised that he was asleep.

She could feel him breathing steadily and, as she took her fingers away, he did not move.

She knew then definitely that he had fallen into a deep and healing sleep.

So she then walked silently across the room in her bedroom slippers and at the door she turned the handle without making any noise.

She was not surprised to see that the door of the boudoir was open.

As she closed the Marquis's door, Hignet appeared.

She put her finger to her lips to show him that the Marquis was asleep and he nodded.

Without speaking he opened the door into the corridor and she slipped through it.

As she moved away, she heard the slight click, which told her that Hignet had locked the door behind her.

She had nearly reached her own room, guided by the light of two candles left burning in their silver sconces and she guessed that Hignet had left them burning since there were two newcomers in the house.

Suddenly she heard the door of the State room opposite hers opening, which was where Lady Isabel was sleeping.

She came out with her dark hair streaming over her shoulders.

She was wearing a flame-coloured *negligée* decorated with lace and velvet bows.

When she saw Erlina, she started and then screamed angrily,

"Where have you been? What are you doing with his Lordship?"

"His Lordship is asleep," Erlina answered, "I have been treating his eyes."

"At this time of night? Do you really expect me to believe such nonsense?" Lady Isabel retorted. "I am not a complete fool."

"It happens to be true," Erlina countered quietly.

"Treating his eyes in your nightgown?" Lady Isabel snarled back. "You think because he cannot see you that you have caught him!"

The way she spoke was just so offensive that Erlina thought that it would be a mistake to reply.

She merely turned to her own door.

As she touched the handle, Lady Isabel came nearer to her.

"Now listen to me," she said. "If you think you can take his Lordship from me, you are very much mistaken. He is mine, you understand – *mine!*"

She almost spat the last word and sounded so aggressive that instinctively Erlina shrank away from her.

"You may well be frightened," Lady Isabel said, "because I warn you that I will scratch out your eyes! I might even kill you if you come between Michael and me!"

"I have no intention of doing anything of the sort, my Lady," Erlina replied, "and you are entirely mistaken in what you are insinuating in this extremely unpleasant manner."

Lady Isabel laughed and it was an ugly sound.

"You don't deceive me with that sort of talk," she spat, "when I find you slipping in and out of his Lordship's bedroom! Just you get out of this house and stay out! I will look after his Lordship and nobody like you is going to stop me."

Erlina opened her bedroom door.

"I think that is for his Lordship to decide for himself," she parried. "As I have just told your Ladyship, you are quite wrong in what you are insinuating in what I consider to be a very vulgar way."

Lady Isabel gave a scream of anger.

But Erlina, as she finished speaking had gone into her bedroom and then closed the door behind her.

She swiftly turned the key in the lock and she was aware that for a few seconds Lady Isabel did not move.

Then she heard her walk away down the corridor.

And Erlina knew that she was going to the Marquis's bedroom.

She thought with some satisfaction that Hignet had anticipated that this might happen and had locked the outer door.

Even so she was afraid that in some way Lady Isabel might manage to wake the Marquis and upset him.

She stood just inside her bedroom listening.

For what seemed to her to be a long time there was silence.

Then she heard Lady Isabel's bedroom door being closed sharply.

With a feeling of triumph she knew that Lady Isabel had been frustrated in her efforts to reach the Marquis.

She had lost the first move in the battle to come!

CHAPTER SIX

Erlina came back into the house from the stables.

She had gone riding very early in the morning with Gerry and Tom.

It had been a joy to be on a magnificent horse and she and the two boys had loved every minute of the ride.

She had also taken the opportunity to look at the horse which Oliver Mell wanted to sell to the Marquis.

It was indeed a very fine horse, but she thought personally that one thousand pounds was too much for it.

She knew that gentlemen did pay large sums at Tattersalls Sale Rooms in London.

Yet she was sure that her father would have considered that it was worth only a half of what he was asking for it.

However she had no intention of interfering in what were the Marquis's private affairs or even offering him her opinion about it.

As she came into the hall and the boys ran to the breakfast room, Dawes said,

"His Lordship's askin' for you, miss. He's in the study with Mr. Oliver."

"I suppose we are rather late," Erlina said contritely, "but it was such a lovely morning."

"And 'tis good that you can be ridin' one of his Lordship's best horses," Dawes added.

Erlina looked at him.

She knew that he understood how slow poor old Nobby was and also the other horses which had not only grown older but had become weak from not being given the right food.

She took off her riding hat and put it on a chair in the hall.

She was wearing a smart habit which had belonged to the Marchioness. It was, however, rather too elaborate for the country.

Underneath it the Marchioness had worn a stiffly starched petticoat with a wide hem of real lace.

It was certainly very much more elegant than anything that Erlina had ever possessed.

She felt it was sad that there was no one to admire her except for the birds and the bees.

She thought, whatever Oliver Mell had said to her in flattering tones, that his eyes had been critical.

She sensed that like Lady Isabel, he resented her presence.

As she walked towards the study, she hoped that he was not upsetting the Marquis.

She was longing to know if her treatment last night had made him feel better and his eyes stronger.

She reached the study door and then she heard Oliver Mell saying,

"I have written out the cheque, Michael."

"Cranley will do that for you," the Marquis replied.

"I would rather he did not know of what is a private transaction between us," Oliver Mell said in a lofty tone. "Servants talk. All you have to do is to sign it."

"Oh, very well," the Marquis said. "Bring me some ink and a pen."

Erlina walked into the room.

She saw that the Marquis was sitting in an armchair by the fireplace.

Oliver Mell had already reached the writing desk that stood in the window.

"Is that you, Erlina?" the Marquis asked. "I was told that you had gone out riding. Did you enjoy yourself?"

"Yes, thank you very very much, my Lord," Erlina replied. "I rode the horse I like best, which is Juno."

"I approve of your choice," the Marquis remarked.

Oliver Mell was searching among the papers on the desk.

"There is ink here," he said, "but I cannot find a quill."

"I think I know where the new ones are," Erlina offered.

She walked to the desk, opened a drawer and took out a new long white quill pen.

She went towards the Marquis with it.

Oliver Mell followed her with the inkpot in one hand and the cheque he had made out for the Marquis to sign in the other.

Erlina noticed that the Marquis had taken a book from the table beside him and laid it on his knees. In that way she reckoned that he could sign the cheque more easily.

Oliver Mell put the cheque down in front of the Marquis, keeping his hand on it as if he thought it might slip through his fingers.

He looked enquiringly at Erlina.

It suddenly struck her that he was carefully hiding from her the amount that was written on the cheque.

On an impulse she dropped the quill pen onto the floor.

There was nothing that Oliver Mell could do but bend down and pick it up.

As he did so, Erlina looked at the cheque.

Then she gave a little cry.

"You have made a big mistake!" she cried. "You have put one nought too many on the cheque. His Lordship had agreed that he would pay you one thousand pounds for Titus not ten thousand pounds!"

She saw the fury in Oliver Mell's face before the Marquis said,

"Up to your tricks again, Oliver! I might have guessed why you were in such a hurry for me to sign the money over to you."

"It was a mistake, of course, it was just a silly mistake," Oliver Mell said sharply. "I will write out another cheque."

He picked up the one in front of the Marquis and walked back to the desk.

"Don't waste your time," the Marquis replied to him sarcastically. "I will have Cranley do it instead. I would prefer him to help me sign it rather than you."

Oliver Mell did not reply.

He merely walked over the room, opened the door and went out slamming it behind him.

The Marquis sighed.

"I might have known that he would try to cheat me!"

"He has behaved absolutely disgracefully," Erlina asserted, "and I shall be glad when he has gone – tomorrow."

"So shall I," the Marquis admitted. "I never thought that he would find me here."

"You don't think that when they go back to London they will tell your friends where you are?"

Erlina asked. "Crowds of people may come rushing down to see you!"

"I can only hope that will not happen," the Marquis answered. "If they do, you will have to hide me somewhere."

"That might be difficult," Erlina said. "Are there any secret passages and Priest's Holes in The Hall?"

"If there are, I have never found any of them," the Marquis replied.

"Then we will have to think of some other hiding place," Erlina said. "In the meantime, if your eyes get better, perhaps you will want to go back to London."

"Is that what you want me to do?" the Marquis surprisingly asked her.

"No, of course not. You know how much I want you to stay here with Gerry and me. When your friends arrive they seemed – to spoil – everything."

There was a little sob in her voice that the Marquis did not miss.

Then he said quietly.

"We think the same on a great many subjects, Erlina. I would like you now to play to me again if you wish to."

Erlina smiled at him.

"I would love to do that," she answered, "if you will just allow me five minutes to eat my breakfast."

"You have not eaten?" the Marquis asked. "I thought, of course, that you would have had breakfast before you went riding."

"I was in too much of a hurry to go to the stables," Erlina answered. "But I promise I will not keep you waiting more than five minutes and I will ask Hignet to take you to the Music Room."

She jumped up and hurried out of the study.

She reached the breakfast room to find the two boys eating some delicious dishes that Mrs. Dawes had prepared.

It was so different from the one egg that was the most Gerry had been able to have in the old days at Sherwood House. Sometimes there was nothing but toast without any butter.

For Tom things had been very much the same and, as he finished everything on his plate, he said in a heartfelt tone,

"I hope his Lordship stays here for ever and ever. Then we can ride his horses and eat his scrumptious food!"

"That is what I say it is too," Gerry chimed in.

Erlina could but not agree with the two boys.

She had been afraid that when his cousin and Lady Isabel had arrived that the Marquis would not want them in the house.

Or he might have decided to go back to his house in London.

She felt strongly that she must keep her fingers crossed and pray that he would still want her services as he needed them now.

She ate quickly and, having told the boys what they were to do, she then ran to the Music Room.

The Marquis was waiting for her and he was sitting at the open window where he had sat yesterday.

Without speaking, she went straight to the piano.

She sat down and started to play whatever came into her mind first.

There was her joy because he had let her try to heal his eyes and because he liked her playing to him.

She went on to tell him how happy she was that he was putting right everything that had gone wrong.

She was pleased that people were returning to the village and men were working on the land and in the garden.

The music went on to tell him that the house was looking clean and beautiful as it had been in the past.

She poured it all out of her heart.

Only when she had played for a long time did she think that perhaps the Marquis might be becoming bored.

She took her hands from the keys and put them in her lap.

For what seemed to her like a long time he did not speak.

Then he began quietly,

"Thank you, Erlina. That is just what I want you to feel."

"You – understood what I – was saying in my music?" she asked.

"I think by now that you realise that I not only understand but I feel the same way," he answered.

She made a little murmur of delight.

Then she walked across the room to his chair and, without asking, bent to put her hands over his eyes.

It was not quite the same as when last night she had been able to try to heal him without the bandage.

Still, as she prayed, she felt uplifted.

And she knew that he was seeing the strong light that would heal him of his blindness.

*

It was luncheontime before Lady Isabel appeared.

Erlina was glad that everybody was assembled in the drawing room and that she was not alone.

She was quiet during the meal while Lady Isabel was quite determined to monopolise the Marquis.

Oliver Mell was sulky because he had been exposed over the cheque.

After he left the Music Room, the Marquis had given Mr. Cranley orders to write out a cheque for one thousand pounds.

When he had signed it, he told him to give it to his cousin.

Erlina knew at once by the expression on Mr. Cranley's face that he disapproved of the transaction.

However it was not his business to comment on it and in fact he brought in some good news as he had found another firm of builders who were prepared to start work in the village immediately.

He also had two more housemaids and another footman moving into The Hall the next day.

"They are all young, my Lord, and prepared to work very hard," Mr. Cranley told the Marquis, "and I hope to find a housekeeper the next time I go to Boxstead."

"I doubt if anyone could run the house better than Miss Sherwood," the Marquis said, "and we need a lot more staff to get the place really clean. I can only beg you, Cranley, to go on collecting them."

"I am doing my utmost best, my Lord," Mr. Cranley replied.

There was another farmer coming after luncheon to talk to the Marquis about renting one of the outlying farms and the Marquis had arranged to see him in the study.

Erlina was for the moment all alone in the drawing room and she was just thinking that there was quite a lot of cleaning still to be done when Gerry came running into the room.

"Tom has had to go home," he said. "His mother wants him this afternoon."

"Then what are you going to do?" Erlina asked.

"I am going to look at the exciting secret that the Marquis told me about."

"That will keep you busy," she commented.

Gerry hurried away and Erlina sat down to look at a book that she had recently noticed in the library.

It was about an intrepid explorer who had visited India and reached as far as the foothills of the Himalayas. And there was a long description of the people that he had met, many of them being Gurus, Sooth-Sayers and, of course, Healers.

He described in some detail just how successful the Healers were with the people of their region and they often travelled long distances to cure their patients

What interested Erlina particularly was how they worked to heal the sight of children as well as old people.

She was deeply into the book when Gerry came bursting into the room.

"Come with me, Erlina!" he begged her. Come with me at once. I have something really amazing to show you!"

"What is it?" Erlina asked, putting down her book reluctantly.

"It's the secret his Lordship told me about and he said, if I wanted to, I could tell you."

"Did he really?" Erlina queried.

Gerry nodded.

Then he put both his hands out and pulled her towards the door.

"Come on, come on," he urged. "It's very very exciting!"

They then went out into the garden and, walking over the still unkempt lawn, they passed through a large clump of rhododendron bushes.

Gerry climbed ahead up a steep twisting path until they came to what Erlina saw was a summer house.

It was a very attractive one, although the paint on the windows had peeled away.

When she looked inside, she saw that there were leaves on the floor which had blown in during the autumn.

There was a wooden seat on which the cushions were faded and torn badly with age.

"Is this what you have found?" she asked.

"Come – come with me," Gerry persisted.

He took her round to the back of the summer house as she wondered just what the secret could possibly be.

Then Gerry started to climb up the side of it.

Erlina saw that there were iron footholds on what must have been the trunk of a tree.

"Follow me, follow me," Gerry urged her.

Because Erlina understood now what this was all about she climbed up after him.

On the top of the summer house there was an aperture that was not noticeable from the front of the building.

It opened into the space inside between the floorboards and the top of the roof, which was pointed.

It was this hiding place that the Marquis had described to Gerry, which as a boy he had obviously used himself.

There was a number of things in it which he must have kept there and they had remained undiscovered after he had grown up.

There were horseshoes that he had collected in the stables and some rough carvings that he might have done himself.

There were several whistles, a huntsman's horn and a riding crop and some very tattered books that looked as if they had been nibbled by mice.

It was a perfect hiding place for a small boy who wanted to escape from his Nanny or his Tutors.

"His Lordship told me that he used to hide here," Gerry was saying, "and, although they called and called for him, no one ever found out where he was hiding."

Erlina sat down on the floor.

Gerry could stand up, although he had to bend his head except in the centre of the floor, but Erlina was too tall to do anything but sit down.

"I think it is a very nice place for you to have all to yourself," she said, "and tomorrow I will clean it out for you."

"I thought that was what you would say," Gerry replied. "I'll help you and will bring up my bow and arrows and some of the other things I found in the attics."

"That is a very good idea," Erlina agreed.

She thought it important for him to have a place that he could call his own and where he could put all his little treasures.

Gerry was thinking it out.

"I will ask Mrs. Dawes," he said, "if she will give me a tin of biscuits, which I can eat up here when I am feeling hungry."

"I am sure she will," Erlina said, "and, as the rug on the floor is rather dirty, we might find a new one and also some cushions to sit on."

"That is a spiffing idea," Gerry approved.

Erlina pulled back the rug from the floor as she spoke and she saw then that the boards beneath it had shrunk a little over the years.

It was easy therefore to look down into the summer house itself.

It was, however, quite safe as the boards rested on heavy beams that were, she reckoned, indestructible.

She was thinking that there were plenty of things in the house that she and Gerry could bring out here.

Suddenly she heard someone speaking below.

She looked down through the crack between the boards.

To her considerable surprise she saw that it was Oliver Mell and Lady Isabel who were standing below them.

Gerry saw them too and Erlina put her finger to her lips to warn him not to speak.

Then she knew that her warning was unnecessary because he would certainly not want them to be aware of his secret hiding place.

In fact he sat down on the floor, taking care not to make a noise with his feet.

"I brought you here," Oliver Mell was saying, "because I have to talk to you and I am always afraid that Michael's accursed servants are listening at the doors."

"You are so right," Lady Isabel agreed, "and that valet of his is always creeping about."

"I have told you that the *damned* girl has prevented me from getting a little money out of Michael," Oliver Mell went on. "It is just like her to walk in through the door at the most awkward moment."

"She would do that," Lady Isabel said spitefully, "and the sooner we get rid of her the better!"

"What we have to do first," Oliver Mell reminded her, "is to get rid of Michael."

"I know that," Lady Isabel said, "but you were not very successful the first time you tried it."

"Anybody else," Oliver Mell fumed, "would have fallen from his horse when the branch struck him across the face and would have been kicked by the animal and ended up by being killed!"

"But none of those things has yet happened," Lady Isabel replied, "and what is more, Michael believes that he will soon be able to see again."

"That is something that has to be prevented," Oliver Mell said. "You do realise, Isabel, that unless I can settle my debts, I will end up in a debtor's prison?"

Lady Isabel gave a little cry.

"Oh, darling, that cannot happen to you."

"I know, I know and it is only Michael who stands between me and an enormous fortune. He is as rich as Croesus!"

The greedy note in his voice was very unpleasant.

"He is also preventing you from being the Marquis of Meldon," Lady Isabel said softly.

"That is true," Oliver Mell said testily. "That is why we have to get rid of him before we leave tomorrow morning."

"I wonder what excuse we could make for staying on here?" Lady Isabel murmured.

"My excuse will be that I have to attend my cousin's funeral," Oliver Mell retorted.

"But how? How?" Lady Isabel asked.

Oliver Mell put his arm around her and pulled her down onto the wooden seat.

"Now listen to what I have planned," he said, "and, once we leave the summer house, we must not speak of it again."

"I am listening," Lady Isabel responded eagerly.

"I have brought with me a very strong poison," Oliver Mell said, "which when put into a man's wine makes him appear to be very drunk."

"You will give it to him at dinner?" Lady Isabel asked.

"That is my intention. Then Michael will appear drunk, very very drunk, so much so that he will have to be helped if not carried upstairs to bed."

Lady Isabel drew in her breath.

"What then?" she asked nervously.

"As I have told you before, his bedroom has a very special window, which was put in by Michael's grandfather. It would be very easy for a man, especially if he was drunk, to fall out of it. And that is what Michael will do!"

He spoke quietly, but there was a note of elation in his voice.

It was as if he was relishing the whole idea of his cousin's dramatic death.

"It sounds all right," Lady Isabel said slowly.

"It is fool proof," Oliver Mell assured her. "Do you not see? No one can connect me with it. Michael gets drunk at dinner and because he is blind falls out of the window."

He looked at her to see if she was understanding what he was saying before he went on,

"He will break his neck when he falls onto the terrace from that window and nobody can possibly be blamed for a mistake made by a blind man."

"You are really very clever, darling," Lady Isabel said in her cooing voice. "I shall enjoy being the Marchioness of Meldon and having unlimited money to spend in London in all the very best shops in Bond Street."

"Just as I shall enjoy myself being the Marquis of Meldon after being pushed off with a mere pittance to call my own," Oliver Mell bragged fervently.

"All that will be changed after tomorrow," Lady Isabel said. "And don't let there be any mistakes. After all you were certain that he would be killed in that ridiculous Steeplechase."

"Instead of which poor old Philip died," Oliver Mell murmured.

"There is nothing you can do about that now," Lady Isabel remarked, "and I think we ought to be going back now."

"I had to tell you what I was doing," Oliver Mell said. "You must go on appearing loving and concerned about him to impress the servants."

"I thought I was doing that act rather well," Lady Isabel answered.

"You are brilliant, you know that," Oliver Mell then assured her, "and, when I am not so harassed as I am now, I will be able to tell you just how much you mean to me."

He pulled her closer and kissed her passionately.

Watching them from above Erlina closed her eyes.

She could hardly believe in a million years all that she had overheard!

How could anything so wicked and appalling be planned by one man against another.

Oliver Mell released Lady Isabel from his embrace.

"Come along, my darling one," he said. "Back to work. There will be time to relax and for me to tell you how much you excite me when all this is over."

"Oh, Oliver, I want you now," Lady Isabel protested.

"It would be a great mistake to linger," he replied. "Who knows, one of those tiresome servants may be looking for us or Michael may be asking for you."

"I doubt it, so long as he has got that idiotic girl with him!" Lady Isabel said viciously. "The first thing you must do as soon as he is dead is to push her and that brat out of the house!"

"I will do so with great relish," Oliver Mell said. "I will never forgive her for stopping Michael from signing that cheque!"

They were walking away as he spoke and Erlina could not hear Lady Isabel's reply.

For a few moments it was difficult to realise that what she had heard was real and not a figment of her imagination.

How could any two people who were well-born plan anything quite so horrible as the Marquis's death in such a cold-blooded way?

Then she realised that sitting beside her Gerry was looking pale and frightened.

"Did you – hear what they were – saying?" he asked her in a whisper.

Erlina put her arm round him.

"Yes, I heard," she answered, "and they are such wicked, wicked people. We have to stop them from killing the Marquis who has been so kind to us."

"How can – we do that?" Gerry asked her.

Because she was thinking Erlina did not reply and he went on,

"If you prevent them from – killing him tonight, they will – try again. They want his – money and because he is – blind he will not be able to – stop them from taking it."

Erlina held her brother close.

"It was incredibly lucky," she said, "that you and I were here and learned of their wicked plot. Now we have to be very clever."

"In what – way?" Gerry asked.

"First of all," Erlina said, "they must never for a moment suspect that we overheard what they were planning. We must therefore behave perfectly normally as we have done up until now."

"That is – going to be very difficult," Gerry replied. "I would like to shoot them with my bow and arrows. And I do wish I was old enough to use a gun."

"Then we would be criminals," Erlina told him, "so we must not do anything wrong and certainly not kill anyone."

"Then how will we stop them from – killing – the Marquis?" Gerry asked again.

Erlina knew as she held him close that he was frightened.

She thought that it was not surprising for she too felt desperately afraid of Oliver Mell.

She was quite certain that he would not hesitate to dispose of them both if he learnt that they knew his dastardly secret.

But how could she allow anyone so despicable and so evil to kill a man like the Marquis?

Even as she asked herself the question she remembered how she herself had hated the Marquis in the first place. She had actually hoped that he would die a miserable death.

Now she knew that she would do anything rather than let him lose his life.

Quite suddenly, like a flash of lightning, she knew that she loved him.

She could hardly believe that it was true.

Yet, as she walked back hand-in-hand with Gerry and, keeping to the shrubs, she knew that she would rather die herself than have him suffer any more.

Now she had learnt that Oliver Mell had deliberately planned his destruction during the Steeplechase.

Because he was Heir Presumptive and would take his cousin's place, he would never rest until the Marquis was dead.

"What can – I do? What – *can* I – do?" she asked herself frantically.

She knew by the way that Gerry was holding onto her hand that he was afraid she would not find an answer.

They reached the house.

Instead of going in by the front door they entered by one of the garden doors.

In this way Erlina hoped to avoid any confrontation with Oliver Mell or Lady Isabel.

They went side by side up a secondary staircase to Gerry's bedroom.

When they were inside, Gerry put his arms round Erlina's neck and hid his face against her shoulder.

"I am – frightened, Erlina," he said. "Frightened they will – kill the Marquis! And you – heard what they said they would do to us!"

Erlina drew her brother down so that they both sat on the bed.

"Now listen to me, Gerry, we have to stay very calm and not in any way make Oliver Mell suspicious that we are watching him or make him feel that anything has changed since yesterday."

She saw that Gerry was listening closely to her and then she went on,

"I want you to stay in your room while I go down and see if I can talk to the Marquis."

"Will you tell him?" Gerry asked.

"I have got to prevent him from drinking the poison that Oliver Mell intends to put into his wine tonight."

She paused and then went on,

"But it would be a mistake for him to get so angry that he accuses his cousin of trying to murder him."

She thought for a moment.

Then she said,

"You were right when you said that if they fail again this time they will go on trying. We have to do something to prevent Oliver Mell from coming anywhere near his Lordship from now on."

Erlina was trying to sort things out in her mind.

Then she asked Gerry,

"Would you be happier if you went to the Vicarage and asked if you could stay the night with Tom? I feel sure that they would be pleased to have you."

Gerry looked at his sister and she knew that he was turning the question over in his mind.

Then, as if he suddenly became grown up, he declared,

"I think, Erlina, I ought to stay with you. After all I am a man and I have to look after you because you are only a woman."

Erlina felt the tears come into her eyes as she bent forward to kiss his cheek.

"That is very brave of you," she told him, "and I know that it is exactly what Papa would have said."

"Papa would have said that I must fight for what is right and good," Gerry remarked, "and Mr. Mell is a bad and wicked man."

"Then we will fight him together!" Erlina claimed.

She wiped her tears away and kissed Gerry again.

"Now you stay here," she said, "while I go to find out what is happening. Will you be all right?"

"I think that I will go up to the attic," Gerry said, "and bring down one of those duelling pistols."

Erlina thought that it was a good idea and could do no harm.

"All right," she said, "and look and see if there is anything else you want to take up to your secret hiding place."

She hoped as she spoke that it would remain a secret place for Gerry for a long time.

If Oliver Mell found out it existed, Gerry would never be able to go there again.

They left the bedroom together and Erlina went along the corridor towards the stairs.

Gerry walked in the opposite direction towards the North wing.

Slowly, because she too was feeling atraid, Erlina went down the stairs.

Dawes was in the hall instructing a new footman on how he should behave when he was on duty.

She passed them by without speaking and walked towards the study.

Just before she reached the door, Mr. Cranley came out of the room.

With him was a tall strong-looking man whom she guessed must be the farmer who had come to be interviewed by the Marquis.

"Good afternoon, Miss Sherwood," Mr. Cranley greeted her.

"Good afternoon, Mr. Cranley," Erlina replied. "Is his Lordship alone?"

"Yes, we have finished our interview and it has all been most satisfactory," Mr. Cranley replied.

"I am so glad," Erlina smiled.

She opened the study door and saw the Marquis sitting in his favourite armchair.

For a moment she forgot everything except that he looked so handsome, so strong and so very attractive and that she loved him.

There was only the black bandage over his eyes to spoil the perfect picture.

She wanted more than anything else to run across to him and then tell him how much he meant to her.

She remembered that what she meant to him was sadly very little.

She was useful in helping him with the house and he believed that in some miraculous way she could cure his blindness.

If she did so, he could be extremely grateful to her.

She could not recall his showing her in any way that he thought of her as an attractive woman.

Or indeed as a woman at all.

He had been concerned only with what she could do to help him with his problems and he had worried about how his friends would now see him.

But she was not important enough for him to worry about how he might appear to her as a blind man.

It all passed swiftly through her mind.

If she showed the Marquis that she was one of what Hignet had called 'the bees round a honeypot' he might easily despise her.

"Them never lasts long!" Hignet had articulated.

Erlina must have stood just inside the door for only a few seconds and yet it seemed to her that a century of thoughts had passed through her mind.

Now she felt as if there was a stone in her breast instead of her heart.

"Is that you, Erlina?" the Marquis asked.

"Yes, it is, my Lord," she answered. "I gather your interview was a great success."

"That farmer is a nice man. I am sure that he will do well. I have let him the farm at quite a reasonable rent."

"I am so glad," Erlina said. "Now we shall no longer see all those fields going to waste."

She spoke without thinking.

"*See* them going to waste?" the Marquis repeated. "That is the operative word is it not, Erlina? Will I be able to see them or will you just have to tell me about them?"

"You *will* see them!" Erlina asserted. "I promise you that."

It was more of a vow than a promise.

She told herself that she would kill Oliver Mell herself rather than let him murder the Marquis.

CHAPTER SEVEN

Erlina walked closer to the Marquis.

And in a voice that he could hardly hear she suggested,

"Will you – come into – the Music Room? I have – something to – tell you."

The Marquis raised his eyebrows.

"The Music Room?" he questioned reflectively.

Erlina did not answer.

She merely waited as he rose to his feet and he then put his hand on her shoulder in the same way that he did when Gerry guided him.

It was the first time that he had done so.

Erlina felt herself thrill because he was actually touching her.

With difficulty she managed to concentrate on getting him through the door and down the passage.

The Music Room was at the end of it and she felt that she could safely talk to him there without anyone overhearing their conversation.

She was thinking of how she herself had actually overheard Oliver Mell and Lady Isabel plotting to murder the Marquis.

She saw to her relief that the Marquis's chair had been moved back from the window to the middle of the room.

She felt sure that nothing she said could be listened to.

The Marquis seated himself, crossed his legs and asked her,

"Now then, what is all this about? I can tell that you are upset."

"Very – upset," Erlina replied.

She went down on her knees beside him and then began her tale,

"I have – something very – important to – tell you, my Lord. You are in great danger!"

"That does not surprise me," the Marquis replied, "but if I am, how have you found out about it?"

Bending forward so that her face was only a little way from his Erlina began to whisper.

She told him exactly what she and Gerry had overheard from the secret hiding place on top of the summer house.

It took her a little time as she started stumbling in her agitation over some of her words.

It was difficult not to keep the horror out of her voice as she was relating her story.

She told the Marquis how she and Gerry had then walked back to the house through the shrubs so that they would not be seen.

"What – can you – do? *What can – you do?*" she asked finally. "As Gerry said – if your cousin fails – this time, he will – try again and again."

The Marquis put out his hand and found hers.

He was aware that Erlina was trembling.

Then he said,

"The only thing that matters is that you have warned me. Now I have to think out how I can prevent Oliver not only from killing me this time but from trying again."

"This will be his – second – attempt," Erlina informed him miserably. "It was he who was – responsible for you damaging – your eyes."

"I rather suspected that," the Marquis said, "and I was a fool to agree to the Steeplechase in the first place."

"But now that – you know just how wicked he is," Erlina persisted, "you must – save yourself. How can you – die in such a – meaningless manner?"

"I agree with you," the Marquis nodded. "It would be most humiliating to be killed by my disreputable cousin because he wants my money."

"And your – title," Erlina added.

"It never struck me for a moment," the Marquis went on, "that Isabel would transfer her affections from me to Oliver. She obviously thinks that he would be easier to manipulate than she found I was."

"It is – all so evil and – wicked that I cannot – believe it is true," Erlina said miserably.

"You should not be mixed up in this sort of degrading situation," the Marquis replied to her sharply.

"But I *am* – mixed up in it," Erlina retorted, "and Gerry and I – have to – help you we have – to!"

The Marquis's hands held hers even more firmly.

"I do not intend to let Oliver win," he almost growled.

"But – how can you – prevent it?" Erlina asked. "And even if you do – not drink the – wine, he may still – try to push you – out of the window anyway."

She paused to look at him before she added,

"He said – something about the bedroom window having been – especially put there by your – grandfather. What did he – mean?"

"I had totally forgotten that you had only been in my bedroom in the dark," the Marquis answered. "The room has three large Georgian sash windows, like those in the rest of the house, which, as you know, lift up from the bottom or come down from the top. They can only be half-opened at any one time."

Erlina was listening and he went on,

"My grandfather suffered from high blood pressure and was always feeling that he could not breathe properly. He therefore had one of the

Georgian windows removed and replaced by a large casement which opens outwards."

He stopped for a moment and then continued,

"As all the windows have very low sills, it can be quite dangerous – and in Oliver's mind a very convenient way of getting rid of me."

Erlina gave a little cry.

"You must not – go near the – window! You must have it – barred or boarded up."

"There is no time to do that before tonight," the Marquis replied, "and anyway, as you yourself have said, he will go on trying in one way or another until he succeeds in murdering me."

"I-I cannot – bear it," Erlina cried. "Stop him – you have to – stop him!"

The Marquis was silent for a moment.

Then he said,

"Does it mean so much to you?"

She was aware that she had betrayed her feelings. Because she did not want him to know the truth, she said quietly,

"How could I not be – really upset and – appalled at this – happening to anyone and especially to – you when you – have been kindness itself to Gerry and me."

"I understand," the Marquis said in a different tone, "and, if I die, Oliver will certainly turn you out the very next day."

"We have – nowhere – to go," Erlina murmured.

"I realise that," the Marquis replied.

He was aware as she spoke that she was still trembling and then he asked her quietly,

"Now go and play to me on the piano while I plan just how I can outwit my outrageous cousin. Perhaps the answer will come to me in your music or from the light you bring me from Heaven."

"It will – I am sure – it will," Erlina enthused.

She took her hand away from his and rose to her feet.

For a second she stood looking down at him, wishing that she could tell him how much she loved him.

Then afraid of her own thoughts she walked slowly over to the piano.

She started to play the music of the woods, the flowers, the birds and the bees as she had before.

And somehow her heart took over her body and so without really meaning to, she poured out her love for him.

She felt that in some way her playing must help him and save him.

She played for a long time until she wondered if the Marquis had gone to sleep in his chair.

Finally he whispered to her,

"Thank you, Erlina."

She took her hands from the keys and he went on,

"I have it all worked out and now I want you to take me upstairs to my bedroom."

Erlina, while he was speaking, had moved from the piano to stand beside his chair.

"Are you – wise to go – there?" she asked him.

"l am quite safe until Oliver gives me the wine that is poisoned," the Marquis answered, "and I want to talk to Hignet."

He pulled himself up from his chair and then put his hand on her shoulder as he had done before.

They walked from the Music Room along the passage to the hall.

Hignet was there speaking to Dawes and, when he saw the Marquis, he exclaimed,

"Oh, there you are, my Lord. I was comin' to tell you that the postman's been and there's some letters, which I've put on your desk as Mr. Cranley ain't in the house."

"They can easily wait," the Marquis replied. "I want you now, Hignet, to take me to my bedroom."

He took his hand from Erlina's shoulder as he spoke.

She felt as he went up the stairs as if he was going away from her and she might never be near him again.

"Tea'll be ready in only a few more minutes in the drawin' room, miss," Dawes said. "Her Ladyship wants it early."

"Then bring it as quickly as you can," Erlina suggested.

She recognised that she must force herself to behave quite naturally.

She thought perhaps it would be a mistake to send for Gerry as even the way he looked at them might make Oliver Mell and Lady Isabel suspicious.

Therefore when tea arrived Erlina poured it out as she always did.

Then she arranged an assortment of cakes and sandwiches on a plate.

As she did so, she murmured something about Gerry playing upstairs, but Oliver Mell and Lady Isabel were obviously not interested.

It was a relief to escape from them and go upstairs to Gerry's bedroom.

He had brought down two duelling pistols from the attic and was cleaning them on his bed.

"I could not find any bullets, Erlina," he reported despondently.

"You are not to think of shooting with these pistols," she admonished him.

"I thought I could protect the Marquis from those who hate him."

"We are going to protect the Marquis by doing exactly what he tells us to do."

"You have told him what they mean to do?" Gerry asked.

"I have and he knows that he has to save himself."

"You warned him that the wine would be poisoned?"

Erlina put her finger up to her lips.

"Not so loud," she urged, "it is a big mistake even to talk about it. The Marquis knows everything and he has a plan, which I am sure he will tell us about in due course."

"He will have to be very careful," Gerry said warningly.

"I know that," Erlina agreed.

There was no message from the Marquis before they went upstairs to dress for dinner.

Only as Erlina had finished dressing and was ready to go downstairs was there a knock on the door.

She opened it and Hignet came into the room.

He closed the door behind him and said in a low voice as if he too was afraid of being overheard.

"'Is Lordship's got everythin' planned out, miss. You and Sir Gerald are to behave quite normal-like and not look worried or anxious."

"That is easier said than done," Erlina murmured.

"I knows, miss," Hignet said, "but we'll defeat those devils, one way or another, so don't you worry about it."

"Are you – sure his Lordship will be – all right?" Erlina asked in a whisper.

"He's too clever to be done in by a pusher like Mr. Oliver," Hignet said. "He's told me to tell you that when he leaves the dining room pretendin' to have drunk too much, you and Sir Gerald are to follow us up the stairs to his bedroom."

Erlina looked surprised.

Before, however, she could ask any questions, Hignet had opened the door and slipped out.

She knew that he did not want to be seen by Oliver Mell or Lady Isabel.

They were late coming downstairs and Erlina and Gerry found the Marquis alone in the drawing room.

He appeared to be completely at his ease and in no way perturbed.

As soon as they had joined him, he started to talk about the farmer to whom he had let a farm this morning. He told them what crops he had planned with him to plant.

"We have to be clever," he said, "and that includes you, Gerry, on your land and grow crops that are not being undercut by cheap imports from abroad, but which are indispensable to this country."

"I don't suppose that anyone will want to farm my land," Gerry answered in a repressed voice.

"I am going to farm it for you," the Marquis replied. "But you have to work with me in taking an interest in what is happening and you must learn all about the rotation of crops and a great many other things so that you will not make any mistakes when you do all the farming yourself."

"That will be fun to learn about," Gerry exclaimed.

Lady Isabel and Oliver Mell, who had entered while the Marquis was talking, heard the end of the conversation.

"I am sure, Michael," he said, "that you are giving Gerry very good advice and this estate certainly wants a great deal done to it."

"I know," the Marquis agreed, "and I am already planning how I can bring in new ideas and new inventions and, of course, more labourers."

He was still talking about farming as they walked towards the dining room after Dawes had announced dinner in his best stentorian voice.

It was obvious to Erlina that the subject of farming bored Oliver Mell.

However, she thought it was clever of the Marquis to pick a subject that involved the future.

She was sure that this would convince his cousin that he had no suspicion of what might happen to him in the immediate present.

Lady Isabel was naturally determined to turn the conversation round to herself.

She began in her usual manner to flirt with the Marquis, ignoring everybody else at the table.

"And what have you been doing with your beautiful self?" Oliver Mell asked Erlina.

"I have been practising on the piano for one thing," she answered, "and then enjoying the sunshine for another."

"You have not been over to see your house again?" he asked.

She thought that he was trying to make her upset about it and so she replied,

"There is nothing I can do about it at the moment, so I try not to think about it."

"How long do you intend to be a guest at Meldon Hall?" he next asked.

"For as long as the Marquis will have us," Erlina replied lightly. "I feel sure I am really helping his eyes and that he will soon be able to see again."

She saw a mocking twist at the corners of Oliver Mell's mouth.

She thought how utterly and completely despicable he was and then, afraid that he might see in her eyes what she was thinking, she started to talk about horses.

She told him how much she enjoyed riding the Marquis's fine thoroughbreds.

"I meant to go riding today," Oliver Mell said in a lofty tone, "but I will make up for it tomorrow and perhaps you will accompany me?"

"That would be delightful," Erlina replied.

She just hoped that she would be forgiven for lying.

It was with an effort that she kept the conversation going while Lady Isabel monopolised the Marquis in her usual unsubtle way.

At last the excellent dinner that Mrs. Dawes had cooked for them came to an end.

It was then that Oliver Mell said,

"I have a surprise for you, Michael."

"What is it?" the Marquis asked.

"Before I left London, His Royal Highness gave me a present to bring you, which I know you will enjoy and appreciate."

"A present?" the Marquis exclaimed.

"I did not produce it yesterday," Oliver Mell went on, "in order to give it time to settle, but I have given it to Dawes to uncork and decant. And it is something really special."

"What is it?" the Marquis enquired again.

"It is a bottle of very fine Tawny Port, which the Prince Regent told me has been kept in wooden barrels for over fifteen years."

"That certainly sounds most interesting," the Marquis remarked.

"It is not only interesting," Oliver Mell said, "but owing to the War, as you know, there is not much well matured Port left in England. The members of White's Club have drunk it all up!"

It was then that Dawes appeared with a glass decanter in his hands.

He put it down on the table in front of the Marquis.

"I am deeply obliged to His Royal Highness," the Marquis said, "and I hope, Oliver, that you will join me."

"The Prince Regent made it very clear that the present was for you, not for me," Oliver said.

He made it sound as if he rather resented that fact in what Erlina thought was a very convincing manner.

"As it so happens," he went on, "I find that Port is too heavy for my taste and I prefer this excellent claret that you have provided us with. But please allow me to pour some Port into your glass."

"I do not like to drink alone," the Marquis said as he did so, "and it is sad if nobody else will join me. Perhaps you will take a glass, Isabel?"

Lady Isabel screwed up her nose.

"I prefer champagne," she responded.

The Marquis gave a sigh and picked up his glass.

"I wonder if you know, Erlina," Oliver asked, "that Port comes from Portugal?"

"My father told me that it comes from Oporto," Erlina replied, "and that it was actually invented by the English when, thanks to the Methuen Treaties, the wines of Portugal were the only wines available to them at that time."

"Goodness me! You are very well informed!" Oliver Mell exclaimed.

"I hope so," Erlina replied, "and in case you had forgotten, the Methuen Treaties were signed in 1703."

"You have most certainly impressed me with your knowledge," Oliver Mell said in an affected tone of voice.

"I too am impressed," the Marquis agreed, "and I find this Port delicious. You are quite sure, Oliver, that you will not have a glass?"

"I would not deprive you of what is a really unique present," Oliver Mell replied, "and to please His Royal Highness, you must drink it all yourself."

"But not at one sitting," the Marquis protested. "The decanter can remain here and I will have a glass or two every night."

Watching Oliver Mell, Erlina knew that he was thinking that there would not be another night for the Marquis.

With an effort she made herself look away and talk to Gerry.

He had hardly spoken a word all through dinner. She had warned him before they came downstairs to be very careful in what he said and did over dinner.

She felt proud of the small boy who was carrying out her instructions perfectly and she was quite certain that Oliver Mell had never given him a second glance.

The Marquis finished his glass of Port.

Now there was a silence round the table as both Oliver Mell and Lady Isabel looked at him.

It was then that he called out,

"Hignet!" in a slurred tone.

Hignet, who was standing by the sideboard with Dawes, hurried to his side.

"I don't – feel very well," the Marquis said thickly. "Get me up – upstairs please – and quickly!"

Hignet helped him out of his chair.

It was quite obvious as they walked towards the door that the Marquis was stumbling and having difficulty in putting one foot in front of the other.

Only as the door closed behind them did Erlina say,

"What is wrong? What can have upset him? He seemed to be so well when he sat down to dinner."

"I think perhaps, he has had far too much to drink," Oliver Mell suggested in a soothing voice.

"Port can be very heady especially if one has been drinking champagne and claret."

"I think I should go to see that he has everything he needs," Erlina said, rising to her feet.

"I am sure that Hignet can manage," Oliver Mell interposed, "and he will soon sleep it off."

Erlina did not reply.

She merely turned towards the door and Gerry followed her.

She thought as she left the room that Oliver Mell and Lady Isabel would be exchanging glances of satisfaction at what had just occurred and that their plot was working well.

Away from the dining room she and Gerry ran across the hall and up the stairs.

They went, as the Marquis had told them to, to his bedroom.

When they entered, Erlina saw that Hignet was pulling the curtains across the windows and shutting out the setting sun.

The Marquis, looking exactly like his usual self, said as he heard them come in,

"There is no hurry. Oliver will not come until he thinks that Hignet has put me into bed and left me alone."

"You were very clever the way you walked in that funny way to the door," Gerry said admiringly. "Mr. Mell thought that you had indeed had too much to drink."

"That is what I was hoping he would think," the Marquis answered. "Now, we must talk very quietly or not at all. Hignet will shortly go downstairs to tell my cousin that I am safely in bed. In the meantime we have to be ready."

"What are you – going to – do?" Erlina asked him nervously.

She was looking, as she spoke, at the window that the Marquis had described to her.

She could easily see that it was very different from the other two.

There were three candles beside the bed illuminating the room.

The Marquis took Erlina by the hand and asked her to guide him to a corner of the room beyond the windows.

There was an attractive screen and behind it Erlina saw that there were two chairs and a stool.

"This is where we are going to sit," he said in a low voice, "as the drama takes place."

Erlina did not understand what he was saying, but did not ask any questions.

She then sat down on one of the chairs and Gerry sat on the stool.

As she did so, she said to the Marquis in a soft voice,

"You don't think it is a mistake for Gerry to be here?"

"I want him as a witness," the Marquis answered. "It would be a mistake for you to be the only person who had seen what Oliver was planning to do to me."

The word 'witness' made Erlina give a little shudder.

If what was happening was brought to Court, she could imagine what a scandal it would be and she realised how horrified the Marquis's friends and relatives would all feel.

However, she knew that she must not ask any questions.

She only sat quietly on the chair with Gerry on the stool beside her.

The Marquis went across the room and had a whispered conversation with Hignet.

The valet brought him back and then left the room.

"I am afraid we are going to have a long wait," the Marquis said, "but at least we are all together."

Erlina thought that it was a touching thing to say and it was what she felt herself.

She could not help being terrified in case this was the last time they would be together.

However cleverly the Marquis might try to prevent it, Oliver Mell would somehow find a way of murdering him.

It was about five minutes later that Hignet returned.

He did not speak to them, but Erlina managed by peeping round the screen to see what he was doing.

He was taking off his coat and waistcoat and putting them down behind a chair.

He next added his shoes and socks.

She wondered what was happening until she saw him pulling a long white nightshirt over his head.

He then climbed into the bed and Erlina saw he was holding in his hand a black bandage like the one that the Marquis was wearing.

Erlina felt that she was now beginning to understand just what the Marquis was planning to do

As Hignet blew out the candles beside the bed, the Marquis felt for her hand.

She slipped her fingers into his and he felt that once again she was trembling.

"It is all right," he said in a whisper. "The real point is we have to catch Oliver actually attempting to murder me. That is the only way I can prevent him from trying again."

Erlina felt that he could not be too sure of this.

At the same time she knew that it would be a mistake to question what the Marquis was doing.

She only held onto him, feeling just as if his strength sustained her although she was still terribly afraid.

"I wish I had a gun," Gerry whispered.

"I am sure that what the Marquis is planning is better," Erlina replied.

She hoped it was, but there was nothing she could do except pray with her heart and soul that nothing would go wrong.

It seemed as if a century passed as they continued to sit there silently in the darkness.

Then there was a slight creaking sound at the other end of the room.

Erlina knew that somebody was coming in through the door and that it was Oliver Mell.

As he did so, Hignet began to snore loudly.

It was the sort of snore that a drunken man might give and, Erlina felt, very convincing.

She could not see him, but she was aware that Oliver Mell was walking slowly, as if he was not sure of his way, down the centre of the room.

He reached the window that was just beside them and with a single movement with both of his hands, pulled back the curtains.

He then unfastened the casement, pushing it wide open.

Watching from the corner where they were hiding, Erlina could hardly breathe.

If he turned and saw them, he would know that he was not alone with his victim.

The Marquis's fingers tightened on hers again and she just knew that he was thinking the same thing.

Now that the window was open there was a faint light from the stars and a half-moon that was creeping up the sky.

Its silver light entering the room made it easier for Oliver Mell to turn round and walk back to the bed.

Erlina knew that he would now be bending over Hignet who continued to snore loudly.

She was aware, although she could not really see it in the darkness, that Oliver Mell was pulling the valet out of bed.

He could not carry him across the room, but laid him on the floor.

Then he dragged him moving backwards over the carpet towards the window.

It made very little sound, just the rustle of silk nightshirt and Oliver Mell's footsteps.

He reached the window and Hignet's face and head were now obscured by the shadow his body cast with the moonlight behind him.

He paused for a moment and then bent forward.

It was then that the Marquis rose from his chair.

"Oliver!" he called in a loud and authoritative voice. "I accuse you of attempted murder and I have three witnesses here to prove that you are trying to kill me!"

His voice rang out.

At the first sound of it, Oliver Mell started violently and took his hands from underneath Hignet's shoulders.

As he turned sharply to stare wildly in the direction of the voice, Oliver Mell somehow slipped on the polished floor between the carpet and the wall.

He gave a startled cry as he fell backwards over the low windowsill.

One moment he was there and the next he had disappeared.

Erlina could hardly believe that it had happened right in front of her.

Then as she stared at the open window she heard the Marquis shouting,

"My God! I can see! *I can see!*"

She looked up at him.

He was standing as he had when he accused his cousin of his attempted murder, but the bandage was no longer over his eyes.

Now he was holding it in his hand and looking at Hignet sitting up on the floor in the moonlight. Because it was all so dramatic and at the same time so overwhelming, Erlina felt as if everything was whirling around her and she must faint.

For perhaps a second or two she was almost unconscious.

Then she was aware that Gerry was jumping up and down.

Hignet was on his feet and the Marquis was still standing there with his black bandage in his hand.

In his usual respectful tone Hignet said,

"I'd better go and tell them lot below, my Lord, that while Mr. Oliver was biddin' your Lordship goodnight, he inadvertently fell out of the window."

"Send some of the men to attend to him," the Marquis said, "and thank you, Hignet. I am very grateful for all you have done for me including just now saving my life."

"I will go with you," Gerry said as Hignet walked down the room.

"You do that," Hignet replied, "and I thinks that Mrs. Dawes'll find you a big cup of hot chocolate. We both of us needs a drink after what's happened here tonight."

He picked up his clothes and shoes from behind the chair and a minute later Erlina heard the door closing behind him and Gerry.

She felt too overcome to move.

The Marquis turned and, putting out his hand, drew her to her feet.

"H-how can you have been – so clever?" she managed to ask as she stood beside him. "Can – you really – see?"

The moonlight was on her face and the Marquis exclaimed,

"You look exactly as I knew you would!"

"How – could you – know?" she murmured.

"I was looking with my heart," he answered, "and now I can do what I have been longing to do for a long time."

He pulled her into his arms and held her close.

Then, before she could realise what was happening, his lips were on hers.

As he kissed her, she knew that this was what she had been longing for and hoping for.

Her love was surging through her breasts in a tidal wave.

With the moonlight silhouetting the Marquis's head, she felt as if he wore a halo like an Archangel who had come down from Heaven.

He kissed her, at first gently and then demandingly, possessively and passionately.

He held her very close and she felt as if her whole body melted into his.

Only when he raised his head did she manage to stammer in a disjointed voice,

"I – love you. *I – love – you.*"

"You told me so when you were playing to me," he said, "and I have loved you for a long time before that."

"I-I cannot – believe it," Erlina whispered.

"I can hardly believe it either. But we have won the battle and now we can live happily ever after."

She looked at him in a bewildered fashion and he said,

"I am asking you to marry me, my darling Erlina."

"I-I thought you – claimed that you would – never marry."

"What I meant was that I would never marry anyone but you. But I thought it impossible for you to exist – and yet you do, you are here with me."

He kissed her again.

She felt that the room was swinging round them and they were flying high into the sky.

Only when she thought that it was just impossible to feel such ecstasy and not die of the wonder of it, the Marquis declared,

"We will be married first thing in the morning, before it is announced that Oliver is dead. I cannot wait any longer."

"H-how can you – do that?" Erlina asked him.

"Very easily," he answered, "the Vicar will marry us and once we are married we can be together and I shall not lie awake all night longing to kiss you."

"Have you really done – that?"

"Every night," he answered. "Now I can have you beside me, my darling, in my arms and, of course, in my heart, as you are already."

"I – never dreamt that you – loved me," Erlina said. "I hoped I was – useful, but – how could I ever – know that you would – want me as your – w-wife?"

"I was determined never to marry until I met you," the Marquis admitted.

Erlina then hid her face against his neck.

"I was – going to try to – persuade you to marry s-someone in – order to – have a son."

"We will have half a dozen sons," he said, "and they will all be as brave and sensible as Gerry."

His arms tightened round her as he went on,

"We have so much to do together in this house and on the estate, beside the other places I own. I will also think of a way to restore your house so that when the sixth Baronet wants to be married he has somewhere to live."

Erlina gave a cry.

"Only – you could – think like that. Only – you would be – so kind and so wonderful to Gerry and me. Tell me I am not – dreaming. Tell me we will – never wake up."

The Marquis looked down at her.

Now, as the moonlight grew stronger, he thought that no one could look more beautiful.

No woman had ever looked more radiant with the ecstasy of love.

"I love you and I worship you," he said. "This is the beginning, my precious, of a new life. You must help me never to hurt people again."

"I know now that – you did not realise what – you were doing," Erlina murmured.

"We will make what reparation we can, you and I," the Marquis said, "and we will make this house a happy home for ourselves, our children and anyone else who stays with us in it."

"That is – what I want – that is what I have always wanted," Erlina said, "but I am afraid – you may be bored with me."

"How could I ever be bored with you?" the Marquis demanded. "And doubtless you will tell me what to do, not only with words but with your music and, of course, with your heart."

"I will – do that – you know I will do it," Erlina answered. "Oh, darling Michael, I love you – I love you and there are no other words in which to – tell you how – wonderful it is that, thanks to God – your eyes are now – healed."

"Thanks to God – and to you, my loved one" the Marquis smiled. "And that, my precious wife-to-be, is the Magic of Love!"

Then he was kissing Erlina again.

She knew as they touched the stars that their love, like the light that had healed his eyes, had come from God.

It would protect, guide and inspire them now and for all Eternity.

OTHER BOOKS IN THIS SERIES

The Barbara Cartland Eternal Collection is the unique opportunity to collect all five hundred of the timeless beautiful romantic novels written by the world's most celebrated and enduring romantic author.

Named the Eternal Collection because Barbara's inspiring stories of pure love, just the same as love itself, the books will be published on the internet at the rate of four titles per month until all five hundred are available.

The Eternal Collection, classic pure romance available worldwide for all time.